Old Pap Stories.

told by a grandpa

about his grandpa

by

Jane Priest Wilson

With Illustrations

by a grandpa

John W. Wilson

Dedication

First and foremost and above all, I humbly dedicate this work of inspirational fiction to my Lord and Savior, Jesus Christ, from whence it came.

Old Pap Stories is also dedicated to my high school sweetheart, John. His loving support, prayers, encouragement and witty ideas are priceless. Having my beloved husband illustrate this book is a dream come true and I am delighted to have him involved in still another way in the creating of my books!

It is our earnest prayer that those who read these pages will be drawn close to the Lord Jesus Christ in every way.

This work of fiction is also especially dedicated to all the many devoted and inspiring homeschool families. All of our grandchildren have been homeschooled and we are so very proud of their accomplishments.

At the suggestion of one of them, we have included a **Grammar Supplement** for homeschool use, as the story teller in these pages certainly *does not* use proper grammar or sentence structure! It is also our prayer that this little work will be of some help to a homeschooled child along the way. May God bless each and every one of you!

Table of Contents

Dedication ....

Table of Contents ....

Acknowledgements ....

Glennie and Scott's Map..

1   Old Pap, God, and Me 1

2   Old Pap and the Honey Tree 19

3   Old Pap, Me, and the River 33

4   Old Pap and Hopscotch 54

5   Old Pap, the Big House, and Isabel 70

6   Old Pap and Miz Dolly 85

7   Old Pap, a Snowman, and the Angels.............102

8   Old Pap, Lila, and the Little Baby Duck.............120

9   Old Pap, Hannah, and the Teacher 135

10   Old Pap, Me, and Huck Finn............................150

11   Old Pap and Roscoe 162

12   Old Pap, Me, and the Swingin' Tree...............178

13   Old Pap and His Larrupins 191

14   Old Pap and Butterfly Memories 196

"Old Pap's Recipe Collection" 199

Supplemental Grammar 201

About the Author...206

Preview: Miracle in Madison 208

Acknowledgements

So much more is accomplished with the help of stringent, meticulous editors. It is with grateful appreciation that I give my complete and sincere acknowledgements to both of them. Rebecca Gunn, you are a hard task-master, but you made it happen! Lara Gunn, your ideas and suggestions have made this project much more complete. I salute you both.

These stories came to me during a very difficult time in our ministry. Actually, it all started with a simple dream. I saw a grandpa and a small boy walking away, down a dusty path through the woods. There were little puffs of dust stirring up with each footstep. Just that simple little dream and "Old Pap Stories" was born. It still makes me smile to remember that.

Each evening for several weeks, I went to my desk and began to type. The experience uplifted me and helped me forget all the troubles of that time. All I can say is that the Lord gave me these stories so I gratefully give Jesus Christ, my Savior, all the glory! Amen!

Old Pap Stories

Glennie and Scott's Map
Old Pap's Place

1   Old Pap, God, and Me

"And he said, "Lord, I believe. And he worshipped him."
John 9:38

Sittin' here on the big old porch, I can see the fireflies just startin' to twinkle. I can hear the squeakin' of the rockin' chair as I sit here. The mornin' glories at the end of the porch are already closed up tight for the night, clean through 'til dawn. Then, they'll put on quite a show. I plan on bein' right here to watch it, too. The end of another good day is upon me and I am enjoyin' myself.

Frank and Fred was here this noon and we had us a grand time a-walkin' and a-talkin' down by the river after lunch. We was reflectin' on how time a-passes so fast. Here it is already 1940! Purely can't believe it's true.

It is always boist'rous when they's here. We talk and visit and laugh 'til my face plumb hurts. Nothin' like a coupla friends a-visitin' in

1

the middle of the day. They make me feel young, for shore.

First, I rocked just little nudges with my feet. I was a-smilin' as I pondered my day. Then I rocked great big hearty rocks. Nothin' like a rockin' chair on a porch at dusk. Dusk has its own smell as the heat of the day passes.

The big old house is empty now 'ceptin' for me and my lazy old hound dog, Buster. That old floppy dog is a lot of company. He just now come up by me on the porch here. Just to be close-like.

Often I have the sounds of family and friends inside, and out here on the porch, too. Sometimes the sounds come from way out in the yard towards the woods and the swingin' tree. But tonight it is all quiet. I'm not alone, though. Actually, I am never alone, and I will tell you exactly how I know that.

It all started with Old Pap. He was a self-taught carpenter, and he was my grandpa. Mostly he raised me his own-self after Pa passed on, with Ma's help, of course. It is easy to remember him with memories all around the old place, but most especially when I am

2

sittin' in his old rockin' chair. He built it with his very own hands years ago.

He taught me how to build things and do repairs of all kinds just by lettin' me go along on his jobs. For years we did jobs together, or off we'd go in different places to get more jobs done in a day.

I remember the day I knew I was never alone just like it was yesterday. I can still see Pap walkin' ahead of me on the trail, the squishy sound of thawin' ground comin' from his old barn boots. First one, then the other lifted with a sort of suckin' sound.

'Twas curious to me that I could see the bottoms of those big old boots as he walked, takin' step after step a-workin' his way towards home.

Other times in the heat of summer, I would watch little puffs of dust around his feet as he walked. I always tried to walk 'zactly in his footsteps, too.

I purely loved that little skip he had in between the steady steps. Often, I would try to mimic that skip, but no one could do that quite like Pap.

Some folk called it a limp. I preferred to call it a skip... that was like him. He skipped along through the days. And he was always bringin' somethin' new and refreshin' to my young mind as we lived out our lives there in the old cabin on the homestead.

My Pap was always busy a-buildin' somethin' for us or for someone else. But that day we was comin' back from a long afternoon of sugarin' off the maple trees. That's where you go along and put a hollow tube into a hole that my Pap drilled into the bark. Then you could catch the sap in a bucket a-hangin' there.

Sap's for makin' maple syrup and maple sugar, of course. There's nothin' like hot maple syrup poured over a big stack of flapjacks, steamin' and sweet.

But, I liked the sugar the best. It turned hard down in the bottom of the pot after they took up the syrup. Break it and just chew it up. Took a long time, so it really satisfied. It was my first hard candy.

Did you know it takes forty whole gallons of sap to make one little gallon of syrup? Learnin' that just amazed me... matter of fact, still does.

Me and Old Pap walked ever'where we went. Sometimes Julia went along. Naw, she wasn't a girl, just an old, tired mule. Maybe she was lazy.

Yep, she was downright lazy, but we didn't care much. Pap was never in a hurry. Even when he went to town to do a job. He would just leave early to give her time enough to go nice and slow. Julia could pull the cart, and that was right handy when we brought in all those gallons and gallons of sap to cook off.

She never ever seemed to mind pulling that little wooden cart of Old Pap's. Mostly she pulled it to carry his supplies for the carpenter jobs that he did all over the county. Seems like he was always busy.

He was a fine builder and a handy man. He could do about any kind of repairs people needed him to do.

Sometimes, I even hitched a ride on Julia, when I was even more lazy than she was *and* when I could coax Pap into lettin' me be!

He'd say, "God gave you two strong legs, so use 'em!" Do you know that even with his little skippy way of walkin', I never once saw him take a ride on Julia? That was always a mystery to me.

Old Pap talked about God a lot. Iffen he wasn't talkin' about God, he was a-talkin' to Him. I know because I heard him many a time. In fact, he talked to God more than any one person I knew back then or have ever known since. 'Ceptin' maybe me. I learn't that from Pap. I watched him and I learn't. That was just the way it was.

Iffen I wanted somethin', he'd say, "Talk to your Father," or "Talk to God," so I would. It worked, too, because in the talkin', I got to know God.

Not the way you know God from learnin' the Bible stories about God but from talkin' to God just like you would a friend.

That's how you get to know a person, isn't it? Talkin' to him? That's what Pap would tell me.

I remember sittin' on an old stump outside the door of the cabin here on the homestead. He'd sit in his cane bottom chair and lean back against the wall.

Sometimes he would talk to me and other times he would talk to God and I'd listen to him a-talkin'.

It was a wondrous thing to hear him talk to God Almighty like that. Like it was normal. Shoot, for Pap, it *was* normal!

He'd chew on a piece of dry hay or green grass and he'd talk. He never chawed tobacca... that I knew of. I was glad 'cause Mr. Sims up the road did that, and his chin and his teeth was always drippin' and stained. Sometimes, he would spit toward somethin' but mostly he missed. Nasty habit.

Anyhow, of an evenin' sometimes Pap would tell me the most wondrous stories from the Bible. Then after breakfast next day, he would read it to me right from God's Book, as he called it. Do you know? They was just the same stories as when he told them to me out there sittin' on a stump. I really was impressed with that. But, truth is, when you read the Bible as much as Old Pap, you know it inside and outside.

I used to think it was odd how my Pap would say that he had seen somethin' new in the Bible. He would be so excited about that and I would just purely shake my head in wonderment. How could somethin' be new when you read it over a hunderd times? Iffen you saw it, you already saw it and it wasn't new anymore.

Oh, I purely understand now because it happens to me all the time, but as a young'un, I couldn't quite figger that. There finally come a time that I saw something new in God's Book, and then I knew.

I do still remember that special day walkin' in from sugarin' off the maples. It was springtime, of course, as that's the time when you make maple syrup.

It happens after the days warm up and the nights are still freezin'. Makes the sap run. But those wondrous spring days was the best. There is still no sweeter smell than those early spring days.

The ground was still firm underfoot. There was still plenty of snow in the woods, but the smell of spring was in the air.

In the garden, you could see the crocuses peekin' their heads up through the snow. They'd be a-bloomin' as purty as you please, cold as ice.

The moss on the trees was startin' to get really green again, a shore sign of spring, and yet, there was no leaves on the trees. It's purely a mysterious and interestin' season.

The squirrels scampered through the treetops chatterin' and screechin' at us when we got too close for their comfort. They was really makin' a ruckus that day as Pap and me walked along.

After a while, I skipped up beside Pap and slid my hand into his big strong one. He always smiled tender-like when I did that, and my heart was glad.

I asked him to tell me again - for the millionth time, I'm shore - about the day he got his limp. He was patient as usual and reached down for a left-over dry twig from last summer's weed crop.

He told me about the day the big tree fell on him. I mean right on top of him and was it not for the branches underneath, he would of been crushed. He would of been killed for sure.

He always said it was God protectin' him. He said that if it wasn't for God, he would be dead, and I would of never been born. Nor my Ma, either, for that matter. Pap told me that many times all through the years.

That was always so strange to think about. Iffen me and my Ma had never been borned. I just knew Pap would of been so sad without us, because he talked a lot about the joy we brought into his life.

His face would light up in a special way any time he talked about Ma. She was his only daughter, and he shore loved to spend time with her.

I enjoyed hearin' the stories of when she was a little girl and about Timmy, the little boy up the road. He turned out to be my Pa when they grew up. I didn't have a little girl up the road when I was a boy. I often wondered who I would marry when I grew up if I didn't have a little girl neighbor.

I thought that was just the way it always happened. God had that all planned out, though, as He always does, but that is a whole other story.

Anyhow, Pap was loggin' the day the big tree fell. That's when you go in and cut down a lot of trees, cut them into lengths, and then float them down the river to the mill, and you make money that way.

It was a warm summer day, full of mosquitoes and deer flies, and boy, was it hot, he said. The sweat poured down his face and he was busy wipin' his eyes with his big red handkerchief when it happened.

He had notched the giant tree on one side and made his angled cut on the opposite side. He watched as it began to fall toward the notch. That's where you cut a big V down low on one side of the tree. That makes the tree fall that direction when you cut at an angle on the opposite side.

Seein' it was goin' the right way, he started to wipe his eyes. In that split second, it hit another tree, glanced off, and come right at him. He said there was no time to think or even to move, but he did cry out, "Jesus, help me!" as he went down.

When he woke up, he was under that big old tree, and he couldn't move. He said that all he knew to do was ask. So he began to pray, to talk to God like the old friend He was.

"God, what are we gonna do now?"

He said it was like a whisper, but God gave him peace. Pap said He told him to just rest easy and catch his breath.

Pap said how blue the sky was as he looked up through the branches there. The big thick limbs was holdin' the trunk away from his body, and he could see where one had snapped and stabbed right into the rocky soil there on the hillside. Oh, he began thankin' God that it hadn't stabbed right through his middle. He had his wife and those precious little children back at the cabin and he just couldn't leave them yet.

Then, Pap told me that my Ma's older brothers was only small tykes then and that she hadn't even been borned yet.

Now, those little boy brothers was Pap's very own little sons. He was so proud of them. Did you know that's just the way pas are? Well, it is.

Their mama was a young, beautiful wisp of a thing, Pap always said. She gave birth to my Ma a couple of years later, and she only lived a few months after that. There was somethin' wrong inside of her, he said.

Oh, Pap grieved for her, he said, but he also said that God helped him through that time. He said God did that by fillin' the void in his heart and givin' him comfort durin' that hard time of his life.

He said he could feel God there with him when he fed and bathed my Ma and her brothers. It was a lonely time without his wife.

The little ones was so young, and he felt helpless trying to take proper care of them. He said iffen not for God, he would of never made it, but with Him, he was never alone.

When he didn't know quite what to do with a young'un, he'd ask God, and somehow, he'd know.

Pap's own mama moved in with them to help out after a while. His Papa had passed on years before. He also said God was with him and with his mama in a special way durin' that time. Then she passed on before my Ma married, and God was there then, too. God just always was with Old Pap.

That day with a giant tree on top of him, it was just the same for him. He said he had the peace of the Lord in his heart. He knew somehow that God was there with him and he wasn't even a-scar't.

After a few minutes, he got his breath back and tried to move. Then, he found that only his foot was caught.

So, with strength the Lord gave him he was able to dig it loose after about an hour. He got out and limped home. He has limped ever since. I guess the foot never quite healed or somethin'.

I always told Pap that maybe it was like when Jacob in the Bible wrestled with God; he always limped. My Pap shore wrestled with that big old tree! Pap always smiled when I would say that. I always loved to make him smile.

Somehow, this day was different. As I listened to the familiar story and held on to the familiar hand, walkin' down that familiar trail, I felt somethin' new and different. It is truly hard to explain, even now.

I had heard it so many times and I had believed ever' single word. But, today was different… I believed in God! I *believed! I really believed!!* It was the most wondrous thing I had ever experienced.

Oh, I had known God was real, and I had known God was with Pap. I had always known that, but today, I knew it in a real way that I'd not known before.

Today, I knew *God was with me.* I felt it down deep in my heart and *I knew that I knew that I knew.*

I *knew* what salvation really truly is, and I truly *knew* that Jesus Christ went to that old cross for me. I knew how He suffered and died for everyone on this here earth… that *He died for me!*

I knew in my heart that He died so I could say "I'm sorry!" and repent of my sins. So I could truly turn away from my sin. And, I tell you right now that I truly knew how sinful I was and that my greatest sin was not believin' in my Savior, Jesus Christ!

I *knew that every word in that Holy Bible is true!* Best of all I *knew that I would surely go to heaven when I died now,* and how salvation is for everyone and how come it is so important. After hearing it all my life, it was purely a wonderment to me that I finally truly understood! *I really and truly believed!* It was *the very best* day of my life!

When I gave my life to Jesus Christ that day, and made Him Lord over my life, Pap knelt beside me right on that old familiar trail. Then we prayed together for me to make Jesus my Lord, and then we cried together.

We cried just like a coupla babies, and we had the greatest time! Do you know you can have fun cryin'? Well, you can.

16

I can shorely tell you that when you accept Jesus as your very own Savior that you will have peace and forgiveness like you have never ever known. That's 'cause it is for everyone!

We hurried home to tell Ma all about it, and do you know what? She cried, too! That was the day I truly understood what it meant to cry when you are happy.

Well, God has been with me ever since. And that is how I know God is always with me just like He was with Old Pap. That is how I know I am never alone, and that I will never be alone.

My mind comes back to now, and I'm a-standin' here with Old Pap's chair a-rockin' slowly behind me on this big old porch. I see that the moon has risen and it is lightin' up the yard. The lilacs are silvery in the moonlight and their fragrance is driftin' along on the cool evenin' breeze. It shorely is downright soothin'.

I guess I will go in now 'cause the mosquitoes are gettin' purty bad. I stretch real good and reach down to scratch my old hound dog behind his big floppy ears.

When I reach for my glasses there in my pocket, I says, "Come on, Buster, you lazy dog. Let's go inside now. God and I have plans for the evenin'."

The worn pages of Old Pap's Bible are a-waitin', and I am readin' again in Genesis-my favorite book! I wonder what new things God will show me tonight.

2   Old Pap and the Honey Tree

"How sweet are thy words unto my taste!
Yea, sweeter than honey to my mouth!"
Psalm 119:103

Old Pap used to tell me about the honey tree that Hank and Harry found. They was Ma's brothers, and boy, did they ever get into a lot of trouble accordin' to Old Pap. They was only a year apart in age and quite a handful right from the start.

This noon I sat on the old porch, eatin' my lunch. Whilst I sat there chewin', I smiled as I remembered how it was.

There was that gleam in Old Pap's eyes when he would talk about those days when Hank and Harry was young'uns. To him it was just like the day before.

Pap's stories was a delight and sometimes a mystery to me when I was a boy. I loved to sit and listen for hours, and you know what? I think he enjoyed sittin' and talkin' for hours.

So, it satisfied us both, you see.

Hank and Harry was red-heads. I often wondered iffen that made for part of their trouble. I always heard that red-heads was temperful and rambunctious.

Only I knew that my Ma was also a red-head, and I just knew she was perfect. Of course, Old Pap told me things about her that made me wonder sometimes. I have to chuckle when I think on it.

I guess she could take care of her own self quite well considerin' she was the youngest, and a girl besides. But, on the other hand, when she headed into her womanhood she was small and as prim and proper as any other gal in the whole region.

Anyhow, back to the boys. Hank's real name was Henry after his mama, Henrietta, and Harry's real name was Harold, after his Papa... Old Pap, to me.

Hank and Harry was red-headed wiry little guys when they was small, and they was as curious as any cat you ever saw, accordin' to Old Pap.

One sunshiny mornin' they was outside

playin' under the big old oak that stood right in front of the old homestead cabin.

They was about four and five years old then. Well, they purely loved to fashion things with sticks and kindlin' wood that Pap would let them have when he split firewood. So they was busy makin' somethin' important.

They also had Pap's shovel out there, and they was just a-diggin' away in the dirt. The shovel was way taller than the two of them, so they purely had to work hard to make it work at all.

Pap and his mama and my Ma, who was just a tiny tot then, was busy 'round to the side with the washin'.

Oh, of course, Ma wasn't washin'. Pap said she was over on the quilt they had laid out in the shade beside the cabin. She was barely a year old and was just wakin' up from her mornin' nap. She was a-cooin' and a-kickin' her feet and grabbin' her toes like a baby does. Her name was Hannah, for real.

It was before Gram moved in at Pap's house. She lived there a long time, but when Ma was about twelve, Gram took the fever and died. Pap always said those was good years. I would of loved to know Gram, he talked about her so much.

Before she moved in, she would come over real often and make bread and help with the wash. Old Pap told me she'd say, "Ain't a man yet what can do up a whitenin' wash proper-like. I'll be there on Sattidy!"

I remember me and Pap sittin' in the haymow one fall. We was mighty satisfied-like with all that hay put up, from over at Elmer Frackley's farm. We was shore tired out, too, so we sat on the edge and dangled our legs over.

Way down below was the big double door of the barn, and above us the pigeons cooed and fluttered around. Once in a while a feather would come a-driftin' down... a-floatin'-like.

It is the first recollection I have of him tellin' me about the honey tree. 'Course, I asked him a hunderd times over to tell me again 'cause I purely did love that story. That day, he was a-tellin' me about how the Word of God was sweeter than honey. I learn't so many good things of the Lord from Old Pap and I knew that God's Word was very important and I loved it like he did.

But then he says to me, "Son, did I ever tell you about the honey tree?" And off he went with that grandest tale of tales.

Soon I was mesmerized, a-layin' back on the hay, watchin' the fluffy clouds float across the sky. He turned and leaned his back against the frame of the haymow door and chewed on a long piece of fresh hay as he talked.

He had one knee up and the other leg still a-danglin' beside mine. I can still see the afternoon sun makin' a glow around his head.

I could almost smell the soapsuds and see the bubbles as he talked, so real was the story to me. It was like I could see Gram bent over the washtub with a little bead of sweat on her upper lip. There was Pap busy a-hangin' the wet clothes, and little Hannah playin' there in the shade. To think, my own Ma had been a little girl baby!

I could just see the two little red-headed boys a-diggin' and playin' under the giant oak tree. It must not have been too giant in those days, but it shore is a giant now. It stands right proud there in front of this big old house. But that's another story, for shore.

He told me that he had just been admirin' Hannah's little round face all flushed with sleep, as she pleasantly laid there enjoyin' the cool of the shade.

He says to Gram, "Soon as I finish a-hangin' these here shirts, I'd better go see about those boys. They shore are quiet."

Then he told me that when he heard the screams of his young sons, his blood ran cold and his heart jumped right up in his throat. He said there is nothin' so scary as the scream of your very own child.

The wet shirts went right down in the dirt, and Pap shot into the woods north of the cabin there as fast as he could go with his bummed-up foot. He told me his heart was a-poundin' 'most right outta his chest.

He'd cleared most of the property for a garden and such but had kept the woods for shelter from the north winter winds. Now they held some unspeakable horror. They held his sons, and he couldn't see where they was.

"Hank! Harry! Where are you?" he screamed in terror.

"Papa, Papa! Here! I comin', Papa!"

Then he saw his oldest, five-year-old Harry, scamperin' over rotten logs, fallin' through tangles of thick vines, the tears runnin' down his face. He had big old red whelps there, too.

"It's bees, Papa! They got Hank! Help! *Help, Papa!*" The small child fell into Old Pap's arms. As he scooped him up, a-runnin' with him to safety, he began to pray.

"Oh, God, give me time! Please, just give me time! Please, God!"

He handed Harry to Gram and rushed back into the woods, and he was plumb ignorin' the pain of the old injury to his foot. Gram began to soothe little Harry and wipe away his tears.

She hurried inside to find some onions to put on the bee stings. She was already prayin', too, and as she tended the little man, Hannah toddled in.

My Ma was so little that she had only just started walkin' and sayin' a couple of words. She come in with wide eyes and tears on her tiny little face, too. She hiccupped and said, "Pappy?" Ever'one was really scar't, but Gram told her that he was gone back to find her brother, and to be a good girl.

It was not easy for Old Pap to find Hank, the screams seemed to come from ever'where. Old Pap said he begged God to protect his little four-year-old son and help him to find his boy. Then he heard the splashin', and since he knew right where the crick was, he hurried in that direction.

The first thing he saw was the shovel... all wet and sticky. Then he saw the bees. They was ever'where, and the air seemed full of 'em like a great cloud right there in the woods.

"Hank! Where are you?!" Old Pap always got tears in his eyes at this part of the story, when the memories come back so real-like.

He blinked a coupla times and swallowed before he continued.

He said there the little guy was up to his chin in the water. The crick wasn't all that deep, but he had fallen and only his little red head was above water. The bees was all around and he was sobbin' deep old sobs that just break your heart when you hear 'em. His little face was swollen so bad, Pap could hardly recognize him. Then, he started to cry, too, callin' out his son's name.

He ran right into the crick, into the cloud of angry bees, and grabbed up his baby boy. Uselessly wavin' away the angry bees, he ran as fast as he could, and that was mighty fast.

Soon, he outran most of the bees, even with his bad foot. Besides, once the intruders was gone, mostly they went back to their own business.

Anyhow, Old Pap and Hank got back to the cabin and stopped right in the smoke from the fire where they had the big old washtub a-cookin'. That took care of the rest of the bees. Quickly, they went on inside the little cabin with the rest of his little family.

Did you know that bees don't like smoke? Well, they don't, and that is always a good thing to remember.

As it turned out, this was the time when Pap had made up his little ditty about bees. I heard him say it many, many times. In fact, just about ever' time he said it there was a bee nearby, either tryin' to get in a window or flyin' around the flowers, or somewheres.

"God made the honey and God made the bees, but not for little boys to tease."

Right then and there in the top of the big old barn a-sittin' in the haymow with Pap, I knew what that meant, and I knew where it come from. I was truly amazed!

Then he began to tell me about the long nights, sittin' up with little Hank, a-bathin' his feverish face with cool wet rags, and changin' out the sliced-onion poultices. They made a awful stink, Pap said, and they was almost glad when they run out of onions.

Then Gram told Pap to go out and get

some mud made up in a bucket. They smeared the mud all over Hank's body to ease the pain and the itch.

Over the next few days, Pap and Gram took turns and sang and cried and prayed, quotin' Scripture over the small boy as he cried and slept fitfully.

The other children was oddly quiet and good durin' that time. Old Pap always said they just knew to be good somehow. Durin' those long days, he made up that little sayin' and the young'uns all learn't it by heart. They lived by it, too, of course!

At last, they knew he was gettin' better when he began to scratch little pictures in the dried mud on his body. Pap would shore smile sweet when he told that part.

It was days and days later that Pap went back into the woods for his shovel. What with Hank so sick and all, he never went for the longest time. But the very same day he went was the day he found the honey tree.

Harry had told him about it, and as Hank got better, he would add to the tale. But, both little boys knew they had been naughty to leave the cabin, and they would tell the tale with sad little faces.

But that didn't keep their eyes from lightin' up rememberin' how their Papa had saved them.

They had taken the shovel, they said, to go a-huntin' just like Papa. They pointed it like a gun here and there, and they was havin' a great old time when they saw the hole in the tree. It was a big one, down low. Then, they began to poke and dig around, first with the big end and then with the handle of the shovel. Before they realized what had happened, the bees was all over them and they began to run.

Harry hollered to get home, but Hank was only four and just too small to understand all the pain of what was happenin'. He ran blindly, a-screamin' at the top of his lungs until he ended up in the crick, which Pap said likely saved his young life.

Or, I should say, what God used to save his life. He always gave God thanks again when he told this story. He was so grateful to have his sons safe and whole again.

So, for years, the family had fresh, sweet honey. It was especially good on Gram's cornbread. Old Pap wrote down lots of his Gram's recipes, like the cornbread one and the one about how to make fried 'taters to eat with cornbread. That was my most favorite way to eat 'taters.

But Pap's story about the honey tree is why, ever' time I see a bee yet today, I love to say "God made the honey and God made the bees, but not for little boys to tease."

Oh, I always knew that those little boys, only four and five at the time, didn't mean to tease the bees, but I also know that to Old Pap's remembrance, they never teased a bee after they found the honey tree.

I never saw that tree as it was long gone before my time, but I knew where it had been. Pap showed me.

And I also remember that bright fall day with the geese honkin' out there on the horizon, sittin' in the barn, up in the haymow with Pap.

With a big old smile, he leaned over and patted my knee and said to me, "Now, let that be a lesson to ya, boy!"

And, you know what? It shorely must have been a good lesson, 'cause after that I never *ever* tried to bother any bees *anywhere*!

3   Old Pap, Me, and the River

"And Jesus, when He was baptized, went up straightway out
of the water…and lo a voice from heaven, saying,
This is my beloved Son, in Whom I am well pleased."
Matthew 3:16a, 17

I had me a mess of fish for supper tonight. It was a fine, fine meal, too. I have loved to eat fish for as far back as I can remember. And that's a long time.

Today, I caught me so many fish, in fact, that I carried a mess down to Elmer Frackley's farm and gave them to his cook, Miss Bethany, there at the back door.

Now, Elmer is a confirmed bachelor. She is really his aunt and thinks the world of him. Likes to say she is his cook, you see. That way she feels like she is important in his life. Miss Bethany's funny like that, and truth is, she is important to him and he plumb thinks the world of her. They are right good neighbors, too. They was shorely good people.

Was nice bein' back on the riverbank today, though, eased back and rememberin'-like. When I was a young'un, my Pa would take me and my Ma fishin' real often. We loved to go with him.

They called him Timmy even though his name was Timothy. Just like in the Bible, too. Do you know that her name is also in the Bible? Hannah, you remember.

When I learn't that my name was in the Bible, I was glad. Later on, when I got into school, sometimes kids would find out my real name was Barnabas and not Barney, and they would tease me somethin' awful.

But, a-knowin' my name come straight from God's book was wonderful. So, like Old Pap always reminded me, I just ignored them and went on about my business. Inside, I was so thankful my Ma and Pa named me from the Bible 'cause that was so special!

Anyway, we had lots of family times of goin' fishin' and such-like. We would take a picnic and a quilt, and later in summer when the water warmed up, we would even swim. Well, Pa and me did. And, do you know what? Pap would go with us most times!

Pap's name was only Harold, and it wasn't even in the Bible. I used to feel kinda sad about that, but then I decided that was alright because ever'one couldn't be in the Bible after all.

The best part came later… when I figured out he was a carpenter just like Jesus! That way it was just fine that his name wasn't in the Bible, 'cause my Pap was very important in another way.

Anyhow, today I remembered how us men would swim, but Ma would sit primly on the bank and watch all of us a-laughin' and a-splashin' and havin' the most wonderful time.

Sometimes, she would lean against the trunk of a tree in the shade and watch us play. Once in a while, she would holler out, "Barney, be careful!" Pap always said that was just her way of sayin' she loved me.

She always smiled a lot whilst we swam. Then at night, I would remember what a special time that was, havin' a ruckus with Pa and Old Pap, and Ma a-sittin' and a-watchin' and smilin'.

The best part was that on swimmin' days or fishin' days I didn't even have to take a nap, but I shore slept good at night! It was a grand time, alright. But I have to tell you that the very best night-time memory of the river was of the day I was baptized there. Right by that big old rock. I remember that when I knew I truly believed and became a Christian, I wanted more than anythin' else to be baptized right in the river.

I wanted to do just like Jesus done when He was baptized in that big old Jordan River over there. Just like Old Pap had read to me from his dog-eared old Bible.

Gettin' baptized is where you go down into the water to show that you believe in Jesus. When you come up, you are all fresh and new. It's the same as when your sins are washed away when you ask forgiveness. You feel plumb clean, inside and outside.

It's like you are buried with Christ, you know, like when He died and all. Then when you come up, it is a whole new life. Just the same as Him… you get to live forever in heaven and that makes you want to live your life for Him for all your borned days.

That is why my memories of that special day are some of my most precious memories in my whole life. Truth is, I have had some mighty good memories, too.

Did you know that wonderful memories always feel good? Well, they do.

It was good goin' fishin' down to the river today. I was shore hungry for a mess of fish. You can get there by follerin' the crick back through the woods quite a ways. Then you just step out on the stones in the water to make your way along the woodsy places where it is hard to get through.

I remember how the gurglin' sound of the water from the river or the creek intrigued me back then. In fact, it still does when I am in the garden. I can hear it faintly out there even now. I went through the woods to the river many a time as a boy. But today, I just strolled right down the road. It's easier walkin' and lots closer besides.

Early, I was out there to dig up some worms and was gone before breakfast. I did wrap a coupla yesterday's biscuits in a cloth and tuck it inside my bib overhauls.

Buster, my lazy old hound dog, come along to keep me company. I carried my cane pole slung over my shoulder, and off we went. Now, 'tis the same one Old Pap made for me years ago. For a while, it was hard to go back there after Old Pap passed on, but over time it became easier.

You know how the pain is really bad when you lose someone you love? Did you know that with time and the Lord's help it gets better? Well, it does, and that's the truth of it.

Me and Pap spent many long summer afternoons at our old favorite fishin' hole. I remember how we would sometimes take our shoes off and sit with our feet in the shallow water along the edge.

You could only do that early in spring before the leeches got so bad they'd eat your legs plumb up! Those big black wormy blood-suckers was shore ornery. They would stick their mouths right to your skin so's you couldn't hardly get 'em off, they was always so hungry. They purely did suck blood!

One time, I got into a bed of baby ones. Trouble was, they was so small that Pap and Ma had to put salt on to get them off. Usually I could just pull them off, but not when they was too tiny to grab onto! I was shore glad salt always kilt 'em right off. They just shriveled up-like. Always felt like a pure miracle when they done that!

The trouble was, before leeches come out, the water would be ice cold right then from the spring melt. It was so cold that sometimes we got goose bumps on our goose bumps!

Me and Pap would talk for hours. Many times, he told me the most wondrous stories from his life and from the Bible, and I knew they was *all true!*

I can remember late in the summer when the cattails was high at the river, I imagined I could see that baby Moses hidden over there in a basket, tucked right there in the cattails. Old Pap's stories was that real. It made me feel bad that old King Pharaoh wanted to kill all them Hebrew baby boys like that.

But then I could just about imagine the Pharaoh's very own daughter a-comin' down and findin' baby Moses hidden there. Then there was that baby's very own sister a-creepin' around and a-hidin' over in the bushes. Still makes me laugh deep down in my belly to think on it.

I would feel so good inside, knowin' that little baby was rescued like that, a-floatin in the cattails.

I always thought it was funny that the mean old Pharaoh's own daughter saved Moses, and then took him home with her! Then that sister went and got his very own mama to take care of him! What a whoop!

Some days when we was a-fishin' down at our woodsy river, I would tie my fishin' twine around my big toe.

Then I would lay back on the soft moss with my arms crossed under my head-like. It still smells the same down by the river as it did then. It smells all fresh and green and mossy-like, and fishy like a river smells.

They is lotsa trees there along the river but the sky above is always a wonder to behold. There at the fishin' and swimmin' hole, you see, the river is wide.

Pap would show me wonderful pictures in the puffy clouds floatin' high above, and we would make up the most wonderful stories right from the clouds!

As they drifted across the bright blue sky, they would change shapes and then the stories would change. It was a never endin' source of entertainment for me and Old Pap.

That one time we was day-dreamin' somethin' awful when my big toe about got yanked off by my fishin' twine! Yippee, I had me a giant fish!

I plumb come alive, and him and me was scramblin' to get aholt of that line before I was pulled right in the river. What a hilarious time we had that day. That big old fish fought like a bear, like he didn't want to come to supper that night at all!

I hollered that I was *not* Jonah and that monster fish was *not* about to swaller me up! That made Pap laugh outright.

After a while the big fish tired out and we wore out. He gave up first and I was glad that he did before I gave out! And I just about did, too. You know, we was determined and we won, but it was after a long battle.

I don't think my Pap would of gave up at all. No sir, not him. He was a determined fisherman. You should of seen him! So, we 'most always brought home a meal, and Ma would smile and cook it up for us.

Then there is that giant rock a few feet from shore right at the fishin' hole. It is a great place to catch those fish that like to hide by the old tree trunk that is submerged beyond it. That rock is about five feet wide and smooth as a table top when you get on it.

We always called it Table Rock. Pap would jump out there first, hold his hand out to me, and help me jump across. Then we was on our own- for real.

We had the grandest times out there. Do you know that rock could be an ark? We would be Noah- first me, then Pap. It was great!

We'd sit back- to- back sometimes and watch the water flowin' along, and it truly was a boat afloat on a flood, or a river, or a lake, or even an ocean.

We took many imagined voyages just like Paul in the New Testament, and sometimes we even shipwrecked. I'm here to tell you them was the good old days.

Often we would sing. We sang songs like "Rock of Ages" or "On Christ the Solid Rock." Then we would laugh and sing "Row, Row, Row Your Boat." Soon, we would do it in a round-like.

I can still hear our voices echoin' out over top of the water. We would have us a grand time of it. A-laughin' and a-singin' and a-settin' on that big old river rock.

After a time, we even built us a right-smart little dock nearby, me and Pap did.

Once in a while, Uncle Harry or Uncle Hank would let some or all of the cousins join us. Oh, we loved them times, because then it was a wild time.

Ever'one would be jumpin' ever' which way, from Table Rock or that there dock. They was a-hollerin', a-splashin', and makin' a worse ruckus than a flock of crows. It was purely a wild time for shore.

Times with friends and those with the cousins was special times, too, but my favorite by far was times just with my Pap and me.

I don't have as many memories of my Pa at the river 'cause he died when I was only a young'un, but the ones I do have are treasures. Me and Pap would often sit and remember together all the wonderful times at the river with Pa and Ma.

She never went to the river as much after Pa passed on. She always had somethin' important to do back at the cabin. I knew it just made her miss Pa more 'cause we'd all had such wonderful times there.

We had moved in with Pap by then, and mostly my memories of home are in that old cabin where my Ma was born. She was always ready to cook up our fish, though, when me and Pap would bring home a mess.

Pap would already have it cleaned up for her. I can still see her servin' it up, and then takin' the hot handle of the coffee pot in her apron. She would pour steamin' cup after cup of the rich black brew for Old Pap. He shore enjoyed his coffee.

I remember when I was old enough to drink coffee, and how I loved to share early mornin' times with Pap over a hot cup of coffee. We'd sit and blow the steam off it.

Sometimes, the two of us would take our steamin' mugs out on the porch and sit and read our Bibles, and discuss what we read.

Afterward, we would often head out to see how much the garden growed overnight. It was always a mystery to me how that happened, but it shorely did.

Then, there was special times we would walk on the road toward the river. Sometimes we would lean over the rails at the bridge and have a quiet talk and plan our day.

Other times we'd laugh at some long-ago river memory, like when I fell off the bridge that time or what happened to my river raft! But that is another story.

We cut firewood and did chores together. We did carpentry jobs together, and gardened together. The fact was that we just spent most of our time together when I wasn't in school.

That was a good time in my life. But, that was before I met Isabel. When I met her, I started buildin' the big house right away. I just knew I would need my own place, and I would bring my new wife to live right by Ma and Pap. Of course, sweet Isabel didn't even know I existed when I started the house, but I knew that one day we would fill it up together. I was in love!

I remember sittin' alone on the bridge or out on Table Rock and dreamin' of that beautiful girl. Sometimes, Pap was with me, and I would talk about her 'til he loved her like his own. I first saw her at the grocery in town. I knew she was about my age though we was both out of school- just barely.

Her black hair was pulled back from her face on the sides and hung halfway down her back in the most beautiful ringlets you ever saw. There was a purty little yellow bow high up there in the back-like, and she had on a soft yellow dress.

I never in all my life saw anyone so beautiful. She plumb took my breath away. I guess you could call it love at first sight.

Didn't take me long to find out her name was Isabel. I purely thought that was a name right from a love song. Her parents had just bought out the sawmill and had recently moved into the apartment over top of it.

I still don't really know how she come to love me, but she did, and we was married only six short months after that day I fell in love with her. I already had the house ready to live in.

Oh, did I work hard! I would work daylight to dark with Ma and Old Pap just a-smilin' and helpin' out where they could. Old Pap was the most help, of course, and we had us a time a-buildin' the first part of the big house.

It didn't actually turn out to be big until later as our family grew. The hard part for us was losin' the big old pine what grew in back. Had to cut it down. Then years later, that big pine in front up and died on us, too. But our little cabin did grow for shore, but that is another story, of course.

What I wanted to tell you about was our weddin' in 1903. You won't never guess!

We got hitched right there at the river! It was the most purtiest, sunshiny day you ever saw. What's more, we got married right at the fishin' hole!

And, would you believe? The preacher, wearin' his preachin' suit, stood out on Table Rock with us.

I remember how he jumped out there first, then me, and then we both helped beautiful Isabel cross over. She had on the purtiest white dress you ever saw. Our family and friends stood up on the mossy shore.

What a glorious day that was! The sun a-shinin', the birds a-singin', and it bein' spring of the year, the air smelled the way it only does in springtime.

So, right up there after my memories of the day I was baptized, my most fondest memories of the river are of our weddin' day. Of course, Old Pap stood up for me, and naturally, Ma was there. She had the biggest ol' tears a-runnin' down her sweet cheeks; she was that happy.

And Isabel's mama was wipin' tears as well, and next thing I knew Pap was, too. I looked over at Isabel's Pa and he was sniffin' and wipin' his nose with a big red kerchief. Me? I was too scar't and too happy to cry.

Next thing I knowed the preacher pronounced us husband and wife, and we woke up the next mornin' in our very own house.

I'll never forget my first sight of her in the kitchen when I come out rubbin' sleep from my eyes. She had coffee steamin' already, and when she handed me a cup, she was the purtiest sight to see. It was barely even daylight, we was that excited about our new life ahead of us.

For the next 29 years we lived right there and we spent ever' anniversary on the banks of that old river. Sometimes, we took a picnic and had a quiet time of celebratin', and other times we'd have us a party and invite ever'one.

What a spread we would have, too, with sawhorses put up quick-like and boards across for tables. The women brought purty tablecloths, and you never saw so many baskets and pots of food! 'Twas enough to feed a multitude. Fact is, you never saw so much food. We ate 'til we purty near popped. Then we laughed and sang and played games and watched the young'uns swim, and there was always a passel of them.

Some years we would have us a hayride startin' at the church and endin' up at the river for a moonlight gatherin', with a campfire and songs and cocoa.

We had us some wonderful times out at the river, and I had a great time there today, me, lazy old Buster, and God. He has blessed my life and I thank Him ever' time I go there.

Do you know that bein' thankful and countin' your blessin's makes you feel good? Well, it does!

I thank Him for everything in my life, my family and friends, my wife, and Old Pap. You see, Old Pap was there the day we buried Isabel beside the river. There is a small graveyard on the hill overlookin' the fishin' hole.

There are loved ones buried inside the little white picket fence. Pap's beloved Henrietta and his Daddy and Gram are there. Ma and Pa are there and my Isabel is, too.

Old Pap was ninety-two years old when Isabel passed, and he really helped me get through that time. He lived two more years after she passed on.

Then one day, me, Buster, and Old Pap's faithful old dog, Happy, went with the rest of the cousins, all the family, and the many friends and buried Old Pap right there inside the fence he had built and took care of with his own hands.

Many's the time that those friends would stop in for a visit so's I wouldn't be so lonely-like. Fact is, they still do. My friends was there for me when Isabel passed on as well. They was purely a comfort to my heart.

Did you know that friends can truly be a comfort to ya just by bein' there? Well, they can.

The truth is that they never even have to say anythin' about it. I purely do enjoy it when old Fred or his brother Frank stop in for coffee these days.

Also, many's the time they pick me up on a Sunday and off we go to church. Other times, Mark comes with 'em durin' the week and we play a game or somethin'. Or I will meet a bunch of the fellas up town at the coffee shop and have a piece of pie and visit for the longest time. Truth is, friends has been a true blessin' to me through the years. They purely has.

Anyhow, it's plumb funny to think about it now--about how Old Pap had loved that little cemetery beside the river. He took fine care of every grave site there. He was always a-pluckin' weeds or a-plantin' flowers. He shorely enjoyed makin' it nice there.

Not long after Old Pap was gone, me and Buster buried old Happy Hopscotch close beside Old Pap. I'm here to tell you that was another sad day. The old fella was fifteen and plain wore out. Besides, he missed Old Pap somethin' awful. He was never the same after Old Pap went. They are together there, right where they can see the river Old Pap loved so.

Now, when I tend the fence and the small graveyard, I have much to be thankful for. Buster, that lazy old dog of mine patiently waits whilst I pluck weeds or plant flowers. I purely enjoy my time when I work there and talk to God. Buster patiently sits a-waggin' his tail once in a while. He waits, and watches the old river go by.

4   Old Pap and Hopscotch

"The hoary head is a crown of glory,
if it be found in the way of righteousness."
Proverbs 16:31

There was a pup in town today that put me in mind of Hopscotch, Old Pap's dog. I was gettin' some birdseed at the feed store with my buddy Mark, after we'd had coffee.

That pup, outside the door there, must have been a distant relative, he looked so much like the old pup. What a wonderful friend Happy Hopscotch was to Old Pap in his later years.

It was some time durin' those years that I began to call him "Old Pap." All my life he had just been Pap. My Ma, Hannah, called him Pappy, and it just fit that I called him Pap. She was the onliest one to call him that. Her two brothers always called him Papa.

As a kid, I remember Pap a-readin' from the Bible all about people with "hoary heads." I couldn't imagine what 'zactly that could mean, but he so carefully explained to me it just meant a person with grey hair or hair gone plumb white.

Now, Old Pap was purely in the way of righteousness like that Bible verse said hoary headed people could be, because he was the most Christian man I ever knew.

I told him that a lot when I was just a young boy, and he would smile at me real tender-like. But he always said it was right simple to be righteous.

He'd say, "Righteousness is just bein' right with the Lord. All you have to do, boy, is just follow in Jesus' footsteps and you will be right with God. Live your life to please Him and it all works out." Then he would reach out and pat my shoulder.

Oh, how Hopscotch loved Old Pap in his white-headed years! He was eighty when the pup first come into our lives. I remember the day like it was yesterday, in spring of 1920.

That mornin' I had picked my first mess of spring sweet peas. The air was fresh and clean and the mosquitoes wasn't too much of a bother yet. The sun was just up, and it was downright nice how it was all sparkly-like on the dew that covered the green leaves and white blossoms there in the pea patch.

I remember a-standin' there, a-breathin' the fresh air and admirin' it all for some minutes before I picked that mess of peas.

Later, I put the peas into a big wicker basket and covered them with a checkered cloth. Isabel liked me to cover things. I kissed my wife of seventeen years, took the basket by the big sturdy handle, put my hat back on, and headed to Old Pap's cabin. Always felt good to know she was watchin' me.

I remember Isabel a-standin' on the porch a-wavin' as I headed out. She never failed to make the perfect picture of the faithful wife. She was purty as a picture and that's a fact.

Makes me chuckle 'cause I can still see Ma watchin' out the window behind Isabel.

Funny how she always liked to know what was goin' on-like.

'Twasn't far to Old Pap's- just across the yard, really, as I had built the big house right on the old homestead property.

I remember steppin' up on the wide porch he had there on the front of his cabin, and how the third step creaked and groaned as it had for years.

Long ago, as a boy, when I wanted to sneak in without bein' heard, I would skip that step, tiptoein' along quiet as a mouse. In those days, I never could quite figger how he always knew I was there. Ever' time.

Anyhow, that day I called inside to see did he want to walk up to Missus Miller's with me and take her that there first mess of peas. I had promised to bring them, and Miller's Market always paid a fair price.

Besides, in a coupla days, I'd have us another fresh mess. Isabel would cook them up for Old Pap, Ma, and me. I knew Ma would make her special fluffy biscuits for the meal. Made my mouth water just to think of it. Fact is, it still does. I am purely glad I have

Old Pap's recipe collection, so I can make them anytime I want.

There is just somethin' wonderful about that first mess of sweet peas in the springtime. Did you know they taste of all outdoors and fresh air and sunshine? That they are what spring tastes like? Well, they are.

Well, Old Pap said "Yep!"

So, after he took the coffee off the stove and got his jacket on, we headed off. I still remember how his cane was a-makin' little holes in the dirt as we walked.

By this time, he needed it just to steady hisself a little, he always said. "Naw, the foot don't hurt none," but I always knew it did.

We talked friendly-like whilst we walked, just like we had for years. Time never seemed to change with Old Pap. Same walk, same skip in his step, same familiar roads and trails, always the same.

That sameness was what made life good with Old Pap. That was what my Ma liked best about her Pappy, too.

That day as we neared Miller's Market, there was a bunch of young'uns playin' hopscotch in the hard-packed dirt out front. They was a-laughin', a-hollerin', and takin' on like a litter of piglets.

Then there was all them puppies. What a sight they made, a-runnin' and a-tumblin' and a-fallin' all over theirselves. We laughed at the sight, and Old Pap stayed outside to watch whilst I went inside to sell my sweet peas.

I remember how he settled down on the bench outside the door, his cane across his knees. His white hair plumb glowed in the sunshine and a big smile was all over his face as I went inside.

Well, when I come out, he had a curly black puppy right up in his lap! The cane was standin' up against the wall. Right there, where I never thought I'd see a dog for the life of me, was a dog!

Seems he never really cared for dogs that much. Oh, he tolerated them through the years when I would beg and cry for pups of my own. And I had not a few in my lifetime, to be shore.

But to have a pup right there on his lap without anyone a-beggin' him, shore surprised me! I had never seen such a thing. And with him eighty years old to boot. But, it looked plumb natural for that pup to be there.

Seems it and the other puppies was follerin' the young'uns as they hopped and skipped along in their childish game.

This little fella kept a-fallin' and a-tumblin' and makin' Old Pap laugh 'til he was beside himself.

Soon, one of the boys come up the steps to run inside for some licorice, and here come that pup, a-follerin' close on his heels.

Old Pap said it was too small to make the steps, so it stretched way up a-wigglin' and a-squirmin' and a-whinin', tryin' with all its' might to get up there.

As the tow-headed little boy went back down a-suckin' on his candy, he reached down with a smile and gave the little pup a push up the steps. Then it was at the top and couldn't go down, so it started a-whinin' all over again.

Well, by then, Old Pap had tears on his face from a-laughin'. With the help of his trusty cane, he quickly made the two steps it took to reach over and scoop up the squiggly little pup.

He sat back down on the bench to watch the show with all the puppies and the young'uns playin' hopscotch.

The little pup licked him up and down, makin' hisself right at home. Then, he turned around two or three times on Old Pap's lap, and promptly fell asleep.

That was where they was when I come out. I will never forget the happy smile that Old Pap had on his eighty-year-old face! His cheeks was plumb pink with pleasure. I wisht you could of seen him.

Well, that was the day Hopscotch come to live with Old Pap. I thought his name for the pup was fittin', don't you? He could always come up with the most interestin' names. Still makes me chuckle.

Missus Miller was always glad to find a home for her Betsy's pups, and Old Pap was much obliged to help her out that day. I just shook my head and chuckled. So much for sameness... sometimes, you just never could out-guess Old Pap.

That little short-legged dog was the most loyal animal I ever did see. He took to Old Pap like a moth to a wool sweater.

It was plumb joyous to see how he was just the life of the old homestead for the rest of Old Pap's years. It purely was.

He happily followed Old Pap to the outhouse, too. Then, he would sit by that old door with the half-moon cut-out 'til Pap come back out.

Then he'd bounce along beside him over to the big house. He'd sit right on the top step 'til his master come out. Pap would come right through that screen door, and let it bang shut behind him.

Good ol' happy Hopscotch bounded to the woods with him, a-sniffin' at ever' log and ever' rock.

A-waggin' his short, curly black tail, he'd bark at ever' critter he saw, a-makin' Old Pap laugh with his antics and surprises.

He'd go to the garden with him, a-tryin' to be ever'wheres at the same time. He'd even go out to the crick with him, a-splashin' mostly, and swimmin' when he could.

That loyal dog slept beside Old Pap's bed at night, all curled up, but ever watchful and listenin' to ever' night sound.

He even had his own rug in the corner of the kitchen. Iffen that was the room where Old Pap was, that was where Hopscotch was. His head would lie on his paws, but his eyes followed Old Pap wherever he went in that kitchen.

That dog went to the barn when Old Pap would milk his cow, Bossie. She was a gentle, brown-eyed girl. 'Course, we all enjoyed the fresh milk, cream, butter, and buttermilk.

Now Hopscotch respected Bossie, but he stayed close. Old Pap always rewarded him with a hearty squirt of warm milk. Of course, Hopscotch would end up with a happy, messy, milky face. Naturally, when they got back to the cabin, he had his very own bowl plumb full.

Old Pap insisted on havin' a cow, chickens, and a garden, even though we was glad to share with him. He didn't have to do all those chores, but, truth was, he enjoyed ever' minute. Besides, we loved his buttermilk.

He liked to be busy, he always said. He limped along steady-like through his days, whistlin' or singin', though he always kept that cane nearby. He also enjoyed sittin' and writin' in his recipe collection. He purely did love to write down ever'one's favorite recipes. Then he would make somethin' right away.

He loved to keep a settin' hen a-workin' all the time so he always had little chicks of various sizes. Never, ever, did Hopscotch *even try* to bother Old Pap's chickens.

He would go out to the hen house and wait outside the gate whilst Old Pap went in and gathered the big brown eggs in a basket. Sorta kept watch-like.

All Old Pap had to do was look at Hopscotch in a certain way and he'd behave like an angel. He shore wanted to please Old Pap. He purely did love that kind old man.

Now that shiny, black dog did enjoy harassin' the barn cats, though. He'd be a-chasin' them with all his might, just to give them a tumble when he caught them!

They knew he wouldn't hurt them, so iffen they got bored with the game, they'd just stop and lick their own selves and the chase would be over. He'd started this little game when he was only a puppy, and he would bound across the barnyard a-pouncin' like a cat his own self.

Soon, Old Pap called him Hoppy for short. Our family was prone to nicknames, and as time went by, the nickname gradually and naturally changed to Happy. That happy dog made Old Pap very happy and contented over the years.

The dog never got very big- not quite a lap dog, but not a large dog, either. But that dog thought he was Old Pap's baby, I guess, because anytime Old Pap would let him, he would jump up into his lap and try to curl up just like he did that first day, a-hangin' off both sides of Old Pap's bony old lap.

Happy's black hair was always short and curly though his muzzle grew somewhat grey over the years. The only change in him seemed to be that he slowed down some, but then Old Pap did too, so that was alright.

But, I guess the most impressive thing I remember about Happy Hopscotch was how he prayed. Yes indeed, he prayed!

Well, I don't rightly know what thoughts he had in his head, unless it was "Thank you Lord, for Pap!" The thing was, that dog learn't to pray whenever Old Pap did. I never really knew how he did it.

It was the most wondrous thing to see Old Pap tell Happy, "Let's pray." He would bow his white head, and right then and there, no matter where it was, that dog would put his head down on his paws and it stayed there until Old Pap said "Amen!"

It was especially impressive at the dinner table. Oh, Hopscotch was never allowed to beg at the table, but when it was time to pray, he was often invited there, especially iffen there was guests, and most especially when they was young'uns.

He would tell the guests that Hopscotch would join them to thank the Lord for the meal. Happy would jump up on a chair that was put beside Old Pap just for that special moment. Then Old Pap would say, "Let's pray, Happy!" He would put his front paws up on the table and lay his head down on them.

Whenever Old Pap said "Amen," the obedient pup would jump down, trot over to his rug, look back at Old Pap, turn around a coupla times, and lay down.

People always loved to see this trick, but Old Pap was very serious about prayer and felt that Hopscotch was so near human that he oughta pray like ever'one else! So, that was what he expected the faithful pup to do.

He always called him Hopscotch when he was dead serious. The bright animal come to whatever Old Pap called him. He purely did call him a lot, too. He enjoyed that pup.

When he would read his Bible ever' day, he read out loud to Hopscotch, and do you know? I believe that dog listened to ever' word that he heard.

He would sit at Old Pap's feet, sometimes inside the house. Sometimes, they would be outside on the porch where Old Pap often sat in his rockin' chair. Wherever Old Pap was, you would find Happy.

He would sit there watchin' Old Pap's ever' move with his ears straight up and his head high, first tiltin' this way, then that. It was a sight to behold.

I always wisht I could ask that dog a few questions and find out just how much he really knew about the Bible and about God.

It was a special and wondrous thing, the friendship that Old Pap and Hopscotch had. It purely was special.

Did you know that it makes you feel good just to love a dog, and it loves you back-like? Well, it does.

The other day, I tried readin' the Bible out loud to my dog, Buster. I been tryin' to get him to pray and listen to the Bible like Happy did. I guess I miss the old fella. Buster was just a pup when ol' Happy passed on, so I was real glad for his company. But, you know, he just hasn't taken the interest in hearin' me read like Happy did with Old Pap.

My floppy old hound dog just lays there with his head on his paws and turns his eyes toward me when I tell him we're gonna read the Bible now.

It's like he says, "I'm not Hopscotch, and I just don't know what you're talkin' about."

That's alright, though, 'cause I will never ever forget that wonderful old dog that made Old Pap so very happy for the last fourteen years of his life. And that was good.

5   Old Pap, the Big House, and Isabel

"Whoso findeth a wife findeth a good thing,
and obtaineth favour of the Lord."
Proverbs 18:22

Standin' out under the big pines and oak trees today, feedin' the birds, I saw a huge flock of geese headin' south. The wind was a-blowin' gentle-like and the sharp smell of leaves a-turnin' color from another frost last night was delicious.

Geese are a shore-fire gauge of when summer's over or when spring is comin' back. It's a kind of lonesome sound in the fall, but it puts vigor in the bones come spring. It shorely does, I tell ya.

I stood there a few extry minutes, a-lookin' at all the old bird feeders and back at the big house. I felt kinda lonely there, but then I took a deep breath of that clean fall air, spoke to the Lord of my thanks, and shook the feelin'.

As I headed back toward the house, though, the memories just purely flooded into my mind. Maybe it was because of that there map.

You see, early this mornin' Hank and Harry's great-grandsons Glennie and Scott come by with a map. They had to draw one for school. They done it from mem'ry, and a right good job they done, too. I really like the drawin' they did of the big house here.

You wouldn't of believed how good it was, but I put in right in the front of this here book. That way you can see for your own self what a fine map they made of Old Pap's and my very own home-place.

Anyhow, seems like only yesterday that my Isabel and I set up housekeepin' in that big house. 'Course, as I said, 'twasn't all that big to begin with.

Ah, but those was the days. I remember just a few days before our weddin' down at the river, we was busy settin' things to order in the new house.

She was up on a chair with her black hair all piled up-like on top of her head with a kerchief tied around it. There was the purtiest little curls pokin' out this way and that, where they had escaped whilst she was workin' away. She wore an apron over her purty dress and was cute as could be.

She put up these dainty little curtains on the windows and got her hands on some colorful rag rugs. Then she purely had those floors clean as a whistle and she shore enough spit-shined 'em to boot.

Ma was down on her knees a-polishin' the legs of the old wood cookstove we had found. Later on, we got us one of those new-fangled kerosene ones. My Isabel shore was happy that day.

Anyhow, Old Pap was a-wipin' dishes and puttin' them up on the shelves 'zactly where Isabel told him. She had him a-hangin' skillets, kettles, and such on pegs near the cookstove and he was happy as a lark.

Even though she was only seventeen, she shore knew just how she wanted her house right from the start. Downright picky, but she was a perky thing, tall and slim and lithe as a willow limb.

As I dumped in a double armful of firewood in the wood box, I recall how she jumped down from the chair, gave me a smile that made my heart go all aflutter, and bustled over to another window.

Life was all in a whir for me. I was only eighteen, and I was about to be a husband. I purely was about to be the man of the house, and what's more, of the house I'd just built with my very own two hands. Me and Pap's hands, that is.

He was as proud of our cabin as I was. It had a big kitchen and parlor all in one with a hand pump for water right on the counter. There was a real built-in sink, too, with a drain that let the water go right outside through the wall. That parlor had a right nice fireplace, too. Only the best for Isabel, Old Pap would say.

There was a nice sized bedroom with a small one over to the side for our first baby. Isabel had smiled and said, "One must plan ahead, you know."

She furnished it with those cute little curtains, a colorful rug, and her mother's old rockin' chair. It was the same one her mama had rocked Isabel in, and the same chair Isabel had rocked her little brothers in, too. It was in her family for years.

Then, settin' over in the corner was her Grampa's old maple trunk with all the little curliques carved in the wood-like.

She had her cherished little baby things and other doodads all tucked away in there. In the years to come, I would see her on her knees a-diggin' in that trunk. She stored lots of things in it through the years.

At first we had just a biffy out back, but later on we got a real water closet with piped-in water. We never could get Pap to put one in. He said an outhouse was just fine for him, and he didn't want to waste good space inside for such as that!

Though there did come a day that he put that big old cast iron tub right in the corner of his bedroom. How we teased him 'bout that, but he purely did love his long soakin' baths. After he'd had a real one at our place, seems his old bones would just get a hankerin' for a good long soak. He said he purely enjoyed a-doin' that whenever he wanted one.

His cabin was full of memories. I recall one evenin' with Isabel and me a-sittin' at his feet on the steps of his big wide porch, havin' a cup of hot tea. I remember how there was flowers a-growin' right near the steps there.

As we sat there contented-like, he did some recollectin' just for our benefit. We always enjoyed his stories and heard them many times through the years. He sat there in his chair, a-rockin' back and forth.

Then he talked-about his weddin' with Henrietta and their short but happy life together. Then, he talked about my Ma gettin' married to Timmy and their own short life.

He said how Ma had always wanted a houseful of children, but Pa died whilst I was young, and there never had been any more babies. Then he would talk about his and Henrietta's babies.

The stories was full of laughter, love, happy times, some sad times, and a lot about God. Many's the time that Pap said how He was always with them. Especially how God was there with him even when time come up short for them.

He told how God helped Ma when she had only one child, then lost her husband, and how He helped her have a blessed life anyhow. He wanted us to cherish ever' moment as if it was our last, and to not waste time a-fussin'.

Ma just sat quietly, peaceful-like, a-noddin' her head now and then, a-sippin' on her hot tea whilst Pap talked. Once in a while, she would say, "Yes, Pappy, that's right."

He knew. He had lived it and watched my Ma and my Pa live it. He just went along from story to story.

There was others he talked about that night for examples, you understand- but the ones we always remembered most was the ones where the mate died young.

Oh, how we didn't want that to happen to us, but we was determined that iffen it did, whoever lived would have glorious happy memories. In fact, we worked right hard to make those happen.

We also took comfort in Pap's words as he shared how God could make life good again, no matter what it threw at you.

Me and Isabel became determined that God would be the Center of our life together so that no matter what happened, He would see us through.

We just never knew right then how hard that could be in the *livin'* of it, and what a test our very lives would be.

But you should of seen Isabel fuss at Old Pap, though. She always thought he worked too hard and should take it easy since he had already worked so many years.

He was just sixty-three when we married, but I think his limp bothered her. Well, it shore didn't bother him so's you could tell. But I knew the foot pained him at times. He worked hard, but he also took his time and enjoyed life. Isabel was just a worrier, that was all. She was a strong gal, mostly, and loved to get right out there in the hay fields or on the other end of the crosscut saw with me right there at the woodpile.

She'd loved to help her Papa at the mill and her Mama with the house chores, so she was used to hard work. She had three little brothers and mostly raised them at times. Her Mama was often busy with book-keepin' at the mills they had owned, and Isabel was right there at home to help out.

I figgered that was likely where she got so set in her ways about how she wanted her own house.

But, she'd say to Pap, "I'll help - you rest for a while," and she would run him off. I'd just chuckle. Do you know why? 'Cause he would!

She could get him to do anythin' she wanted him to, and it was always an entertainment to me and Ma. He shorely loved to write down Isabel's recipes, too.

Ma still lived in the old cabin with Pap where we had moved when my Pa had died. She always called him Pappy, too. So now, he had two women to boss him around, but he loved it. I know he loved ever' minute.

That day, a-settin' the house to order, though, he was at Isabel's beck and call. He just wouldn't keep still, so she gave him little jobs to keep him busy and happy. That was Pap, always happiest when he was busy.

I caught him one time that day, though, sittin', rockin', and smilin'. There he was right in Isabel's rockin' chair.

I just smiled at him when I peeked in the nursery door and went on into the big bedroom with my arms piled high with blankets, quilts, and rugs. Ma was right behind me givin' orders as to where Isabel wanted ever'thin', and I was deliriously happy to do it just right.

Isabel was the one what got Old Pap started buildin' birdhouses and birdfeeders. She told him how fellas would get the cast-off slab wood from the sawmill, cut it up, and make it into homes and feeders for critters.

One day, he limped to town and down to the sawmill. He brought a load of slab wood home on old Millie's back. Millie was Julia's daughter. Remember the mule from when I was a boy? Well, Pap always kept a mule on hand, even after pickup trucks come along.

Do you know that a mule can live a long time just like a trusty old dog? Well, they can.

I'd see Old Pap headed home, leadin' and limpin' with one of those mules in tow, all loaded up with work supplies or some treasure or other.

Well, when he started buildin' with slab wood, he sorta kept it a secret from Isabel. "A s'prise," he'd say with a merry twinkle in his mischievous eyes.

I would hear him out back of his cabin in his little workshop a-poundin' or a-sawin' away, and I knew he was happily creatin' somethin' interestin'.

On our first month's anniversary, he called to us as we sat out on our steps along about dark. Together we was enjoyin' our evenin', peaceful-like. I helped her stand up slow-like. Then, we took hands and strolled over to see what was up. We wasn't in no particular hurry and just enjoyin' each other.

My Pap had a big surprise there for my Isabel, and it plumb made my heart happy. There on his big wide porch, he had the first three birdhouses of all the many, many birdhouses and birdfeeders that he would make in the years to come.

'Course, Isabel hopped up and down, clappin' her hands and squealin' like a pig under a gate. There stood Pap grinnin' from ear to ear. He'd tickled her, and that tickled him. I'm here to tell ya that it tickled all of us that evenin'.

He declared that they was our first anniversary present, and that he would put them up for her tomorrow anywhere she wanted them. Then Ma appeared with good hot coffee and rich cream, and she was a-smilin' real nice at her Pappy.

We sat on their big porch 'til the moon rose up big and bright. Isabel was so happy that night. Still makes me smile when I think of all the feeders and birdhouses that adorn this place even now.

It makes me happy when I remember how she loved the birds, and how she loved feedin' and carin' for 'em. She even liked the nasty job of cleanin' the feeders!

She had Pap fashion little shields to keep the squirrels out of the birdseed, and then she had him build special corn feeders just for them. Well, they turned out to be for the blue jays, too, as a matter of fact. When she discovered how they loved the corn, she just put out extry for them. Made life at the other feeders a lot more peaceful as bossy as those blue jays are.

I still feed the birds and critters on all of Old Pap's and Isabel's feeders, and once a year I clean out the birdhouses. Makes me feel closer to them, somehow.

Then there come a time when Isabel started feelin' porely. We all fussed and fretted. Ma come over to help out and keep her in bed.

Then one day Ma and her come to Pap and me with news. Ma was just beamin' with the biggest old smile you ever saw. But, you should of seen Pap's face when they told us! I'd give a lot just to see that expression again. His first great- grandchild! He was thrilled, and I about fainted.

What a surprise that was, and what a great relief, too. Here I had thought she was mighty sick and was worried almost to death, and instead, she was gonna give me a boy baby. Of course it would be a boy! There was never any question about that.

I remember whoopin' so loud it made Ma jump and a-tossin' my hat so high that it landed in a tree, and I had to climb up and fetch it the next day. Still makes me chuckle. What a boy I was then, tryin' to be a man. I grew up fast after that. Life will do that, you know.

Sittin' there, on the steps of my own big wide porch this mornin', it was a warm feelin' all the memories gave me. With Buster at my feet, I held my coffee mug in my hands with my elbows on my knees, watchin' the birds and hearin' 'em sing. And I thanked God for ever' memory and ever' bird, too. Even for lazy, old Buster.

Do you know you can talk to God anywhere you might be? Well, you can.

6   Old Pap and Miz Dolly

*"And we know that all things work together for good
to them that love God, to them who are the called
according to His purpose." Romans 8:28*

A-standin' in the upstairs window, I can see
the snow startin' to fall. It has been sleetin'
and icin' most of the evenin'. What a storm!

I am sure glad Frank and Fred had time
to get home before it really got bad. I plumb
enjoy my friends whenever they come a-
visitin'.

The wind is pickin' up and the last of the
leaves are a-whippin' away from the old oak
tree out front. It's plumb swayin' back and
forth, and there's ice chunks just a-flyin' out
there. Things are getting' mighty slippery, too.

So, I'm shore thankful to be back inside
where it's toasty warm. The mule and the

chickens are all shut up nice and warm in the barn. I am glad that I didn't fall and break somethin' on that there ice! There was icicles a-pokin' my cheeks and freezin' my nose whilst I worked.

I was near froze when I got back in, but the chores are done for the day now. I plumb enjoyed how a good hot mug of strong coffee warmed me right up. There's nothin' like it.

I come up here to get those old white sheets I promised the Parson. They will use them for angel costumes or curtains for the Christmas play in a few weeks.

Those young'uns are a delight come Christmas. You remember Hank and Harry's great-grandsons, Glennie and Scott, what drew the map in the front of this here book? They will be wise-men, and Hank's little great-granddaughter, Amy, will be Mary. What a sight that will be with her coal black hair and bright shinin' eyes! Never fails to amaze me to see young'uns in a Christmas play. Brings tears to my own two eyes.

You know Hank and Harry are Ma's brothers, my favorite uncles, and nearest kin these days. Ma lives with dear old Uncle Harry and Aunt Sarah now. Bein' into their eighties and in pore health, they have enjoyed Ma bein' there to help out.

She's up in her seventies already, but her health is good and she has a young happy heart. I miss her, but they do sorely need her.

The uncles are spry for old fellas, live only a mile apart, and they had the most wonderful young'uns who grew up and gave us all those little grandchildren and great-grandchildren. Leastwise, they was like our very own!

What I love is when they come dashin' up unawares, shoutin', "Uncle Barney! Uncle Barney!" Makes my day for shore. I always loved havin' 'em all call me "Uncle" 'cause I never had brothers or sisters to give me nieces and nephews. But, I have a passel of 'em anyway! Between them and Isabel's brothers' young'uns, there's never been a shortage. Truly, it makes me feel like a real grandpa.

~~~

Lookin' out the window, my arms full of sheets, with the first snow just startin' to stick, my memories are so clear. I can almost see

Old Pap and Miz Dolly makin' their way through the storm. So much like the day I first set eyes on her and her four little "granchilluns" as she used to call them.

Oh, she had them bundled up against the cold 'till they waddled as they followed along single file behind Millie mule.

She had the smallest one in her arms at the back of the line and Old Pap limped along beside Millie holdin' another small bundle atop her back. He had gone into to town with Millie carryin' his tools for a repair job at the General Store. Now he come back with a surprise, for sure.

Two medium-sized bundles skipped along in between, that is, skippin' best they could with all their bundles of wraps, and the icy trail, and waddlin' besides. You could tell from the kitchen window they was lively, though.

I called to Isabel where she sat rockin' in the nursery. She spent a lot of time there since she'd lost the baby. Ma fussed and fretted over her, a-bringin' her hot drinks and a-makin' shore she had her shawl tucked up tight. She was so very sad and just hadn't been able to shake it.

After Eddie, our first baby, was lost, she'd sprung back after healin' up, and in a few weeks her optimism made her prepare for another child she just knew would come to us one day.

Her strength come back, and she was busy around the house and in the woods or barn. Just wherever she decided to be busy ever' day. She was such a perky little thing.

Then, the second baby was lost shortly after we knew we was expectin'. We never knew iffen it was a boy or a girl. The nursery was still empty.

But, with the Lord's helpin' hand, she healed up from that loss, too, and as our sadness healed together, we began to hope for another baby, "In the Lord's timin' " we'd say.

For almost two years, we held hands together each day as we gave thanks and asked God for another child.

Then little Bonnie came way early after we had waited so long for her, and she was born without ever takin' a breath. None of the babies was full growed so she never held 'em in her arms the way a mother does, and she never nursed 'em or rocked 'em the way her heart desired.

Then the worst news of all come when Doc Willis said there would be no more babies. He was truly sorry for her, a-knowin' how she wanted a child. I remember him wipin' his eyes with his sleeve as he quietly went out the door.

I can remember how the first spring fireflies twinkled out there that night. I could hardly understand how the stars above could shine when our whole world was fallin' in all around us.

This time the grief was just too much for Isabel, and she hadn't rallied at all. It 'bout near broke my heart to see it, but it took her a long time to heal enough to get out of the big featherbed. Now, she just sat there in the rockin' chair and stared out the window for hours at a time.

I pushed my own disappointment aside, but my heart was near busted to see her so sad and empty.

At night when I held her in my arms, she was like a brokenhearted child, limp and sad through and through. We cried together many, many nights. Cried and prayed.

I just had to keep faith that God knew all about it and that He had a good plan for our lives. I prayed for her and for us, and I prayed for our family that I somehow knew He would give us.

Somehow I always knew He would work it all out for good. I didn't know how on earth He would do such a thing, but I just trusted that He would.

We'd been married five years, and the only time Isabel had been sick was when she was in a family way. This time, with the bad news, too, she was just so very tired. It was like she plumb gave up.

Ma moved in with us durin' the third pregnancy to keep my Isabel in the bed and tend the house. She had stayed on, and Isabel and I was used to her bein' with us and bringin' a smile to our days.

She sang and whistled whilst she worked, and life seemed almost normal. Iffen only

Isabel would get well in her heart. I believe her body was well, and Doc Willis said so. She just hadn't got her strength nor her will back.

Ma and I prayed ever' day together for her healin', for a miracle that would make Isabel love life again. The weeks went slowly by, with Ma and I a-prayin' and a-willin' things to be a-right again.

Pore Old Pap- it near broke his heart in two to see Isabel that way. He loved her so. He tried ever'thin' he could think of to cheer her. He shorely did.

He put a birdfeeder right outside the nursery window, and he whittled her a whistle just like he used to make me when I was a boy. He could make the most wonderful whistles with the most wonderful music! Oh, how he could play a whistle! But, that is another story.

Anyway, Old Pap would come and read the Bible aloud to Isabel. He'd sit there on the side of the small bed. We had put it there for Ma to sleep in.

She had some of her things there to make it homey-like, but the rocker, trunk, baby things, and the cradle was all there, too. I made that cradle the first time around. I had spent many hours carvin' and dreamin' of the son we would have. It just wasn't meant to be, I guess.

Isabel would be polite and quietly listen as Old Pap read on and on. There was a love in his raspy old voice that was soothin' and he said that God's Word would bring healin' for shore. He would often remind her that God loved her and that it would all work out someday for His glory.

Sometimes he would tell her a funny story about a job he'd done in town or for a farmer that day. Anythin' to try and get a smile out of her. Once in a while, she gave a sad tiny one, was all.

Then he would usher her in to the dinner table and coax her to eat. She ate some, but she had no interest. Mostly, she just sat and picked at her food. Soon, she would be back in the nursery, a-sittin' and a-rockin'.

Now, winter was comin' on and I shore dreaded it. She wasn't herself, and winter was usually her favorite time with the snow and all the little chirpin' chickadees at the feeders. She'd kept meat fat tied up on the feeder and lots of nuthatches and such was there makin' a merry song. Isabel's excitement and love for the birds was an entertainment to us all durin' winter.

She always had made a big thing of Christmas with all the family young'uns over for a special sleigh ride and a big Christmas tree. Now, we had a long, sad winter ahead of us. Some days I would plumb wonder how we would get through Christmas at all.

But, that day, with the snow fallin' and Old Pap bringin' company, I called to Isabel that someone was here, to come on out.

I slipped on my coat and hat, and stepped out onto the porch we had built. Now with the roof overhead, we could stand or sit out there rain or shine, or snow, for that matter.

Old Pap was a-chatterin' and a-callin' out before I could really make out what he was sayin'. Somethin' about the cookie jar? Soon, all those bundles and the kindly colored lady was inside, with Ma fussin' over 'em showin' 'em where to put their heavy wraps.

Ma got busy right away makin' hot cocoa and coffee, and hurried and got her big cookie jar down. She had brought her own when she finally moved in along with some of her own favorite kitchen things.

It was the same cookie jar I'd snitched cookies from when I was just a boy. Me and Old Pap, that is. We had us a jolly time a-sneakin' Ma's oatmeal cookies. But, she kept it full, knowin' they'd soon disappear, I guess! Old Pap even put her recipe down in his recipe collection.

The story was, as Old Pap chattered on through the mornin', that Miz Dolly had been at the stable in town. What a place for a lady, he'd said, a-scoopin' out horse manure and soiled hay. He'd discovered her there when he went to repair some boards on a couple of stalls for Smithy.

Did you know that for years every blacksmith in that old shop had been called Smithy? Well, they was.

Anyhow, Old Pap said the stable was no place for young'uns either. Of course, Miz Dolly argued that it was honest work, and she and her granchilluns was thankful to have the little room in back for 'em to live in. With flashin' eyes, she said, "It even had a stove and a lamp and two whole beds."

Nothin' dishonorable in that, she declared heartily! Besides, the blacksmith gave her all the milk she needed for the baby and for the little girls.

Oh, what a sight they was, arguin' back and forth. Her chubby face, black as coal, with the whitest teeth you ever saw, smilin' all the time, even when she was riled and her eyes was a-snappin'.

And, you shoulda seen those girls! Cutest little colored gals I ever did see. They was five, four, and two, and then the baby was about four months old. Little black wiry pigtails a-stickin' out all over their small little heads, with colorful twine or ribbons on ever' one.

All 'ceptin' the baby, and she had tight little curls all over her head, and the prettiest brown skin you ever saw. Her name was

Lila… that was the first name I learn't, as from the start we all called her Lila Baby.

Then there was Lilly May. She was two, still sucked her thumb, and hid behind her Grammy's skirts.

Little Louisa was four, bright, peppy and into ever'thin'. Nothin' shy about her! Makes me laugh to remember the little sprite!

Liza Jane was the oldest at five, and she knew it, takin' charge, and helpin' with the baby and even tryin' to help at the table.

It was a sight to behold with her little pigtails barely reachin' the top of the table and her scoopin' up dishes and such as that. Biggest old dimples, and smilin' all the while. She was purely somethin' else altogether.

All through that mornin', we got to know Miz Dolly and her story, how the little ones lost their folks in a riverboat accident three months ago, and no one knew where they come from or where to send them.

Miz Dolly had been there at the river that day and took them in, declarin' they was sent from God, and as far as she was concerned, they was blood kin. You never saw a more proud grandma. She declared that they had turned her sorrow into joy- yes, they had.

There was somethin' special about Miz Dolly, a-takin' in someone else's babies that way. She had never married, but she had the kindliest eyes. We knew early on that she loved God the way we did, that she trusted Him. She looked at Isabel in some kind of a knowin' way that just made you love her.

We all talked and listened whilst Ma made chicken soup and biscuits. Little Liza Jane was right at her heels, wantin' to help with anythin'. Ma was good with young'uns and was tickled with her and Louisa. Soon she had them up at the table cuttin' cookie dough, with white flour all over their small, black, happy faces.

Lilly May had found the toy box that we had kept handy for Harry's and Hank's grandchildren, and she was happily a-stackin' blocks, lookin' up ever' once in a while to see that her Grammy was close by.

Finally, the baby slept on Miz Dolly's lap. Ma and I was amazed when Isabel offered to take her and lay her in the cradle. You see, there had been many little babies over to visit and she avoided them in a sad solemn way, so we looked at each other with a question when she tenderly carried that tiny tot out of the room, never sayin' a word.

When she didn't come back after better than a half hour, I went to find her. My heart swelled with gladness when I saw her sittin' there in her mama's rockin' chair and that little orphaned baby nestled in her arms. It was the look on her face that told me it would be alright. That we had our miracle.

She held out her free hand to me and pulled me down for a kiss, and I thought I would bust wide open with joy. Wonder of wonders, there she was, purty as you please, with a smile I hadn't seen in a good while.

There lay a little angel sent straight from God with a miracle in her pocket. Now we had a baby in the house for all those little clothes Isabel had sewn with so much love. We had us a family! A real big family, just like I knew we would one day.

Because, you see, Miz Dolly and her girls stayed on with us. The house began to grow.

Old Pap and I started in right away to build in the big attic we had upstairs. We made three small bedrooms up there, and the cradle and rocker went in Miz Dolly's room.

And she had a job for as long as she would want it. She would help out with cookin', laundry, ironin' and other house and garden chores. And in exchange, we agreed to give her and the girls room and board, and Isabel would teach the little ones.

Miz Dolly was thrilled to get them "a ejecashun," and Isabel had reason to live again. Before I come into her life, she always wanted to be a teacher and was smart as a whip.

She could teach like you never woulda thought. It was a forgotten dream come true. So, as you can see, the Good Lord had done it again... turned it all for good... as Old Pap reminded me many times that He would.

Then, that next spring we built a classroom and a playroom on the back of the house. So my Isabel was their happy teacher, and Ma had her room all to herself again. Now, that shorely made her happy, not only to have her room back but to see Isabel with a reason to live again.

Ma enjoyed all the years with Miz Dolly. We all got a kick at how Miz Dolly loved to write down recipes from Old Pap's very own collection. Then she would go and cook 'em up, too! Truly, we was forever grateful that Old Pap had brought Miz Dolly and her miracle home that snowy day. Right behind a poky old mule.

I better get back downstairs and get the soup on. I am plumb gettin' a hunger on. I've dawdled long enough, but these rooms shore bring back good memories of the little colored girls a-growin' up here. They brought joy to our home and a delight to all our hearts—me and Isabel's, Ma's, Old Pap's, and Miz Dolly's.

7 Old Pap, a Snowman, and the Angels

"...weeping may endure for a night,
but joy cometh in the morning."
Psalm 30:5b

Sittin' here in front of the fireplace, I am warm as toast. In fact, with my creamy hot cocoa I just had some good fresh toast. I loaded it up with thick rich butter, too. Mmmmm.

I got up a minute ago and wiped a big circle in the frost on the window so's I could see out. There is a full moon up there behind that white cloud cover, and it is shorely bright out there. Those big old snowflakes are fallin' steady-like and thick as thieves, but peaceful-like. After I turned off the radio story, I spent time readin' my Bible and talkin' to the Lord.

Now, the light is off, too, and just starin' into the fireplace is restful-like. It's not long 'til bedtime for me and my lazy old Buster dog. Sittin' there, hearin' him scratchin' his ears and listenin' to the cracklin' fire, makes me think of a night like this long, long ago.

Winter most always makes me think of Old Pap and the snowman, way back when I was knee-high to a grasshopper.

Layin' in my little bed, I felt very small that night. I was missin' my Pa so much I thought my heart would break right in two.

Iffen it wasn't for Ma, I would of wisht it would of broke, so I could just die and go be with Pa. Me and Pa together, just the way it used to be. The way it was supposed to be.

But Ma needed me now. I was "her little man," she said. Oh, that scar't me then. I was only six years old. Well, almost.

Pa had gone that spring. We had made it through that long, lonesome summer. Before winter set in, we had moved in with Pap. That was such a relief to me, 'cause now I didn't have to be the man of the house all by myself.

She had said it again that night when she tucked me in and we said our prayers together. It didn't scare me so bad bein' in Pap's snug little cabin, but I was just plumb lonely for Pa.

Especially after Pap had just told me the story about Joseph in the Bible, and how he was away from his Pa for so many years. Only thing was, he did see him again, and I knew I'd never see my Pa again.

Well, that same night with the first big snowfall driftin' and a-coverin' the cabin, it was all muffled-like. Did you know that snow kinda snuffs out sound? Makes the woods and all very quiet? Well, it does!

But, that night I missed Pa worse than ever. We would never get to roll in the snow together again, or have snowball fights, or make a snowman, or ever ride in the sleigh together again.

I remember how the tears wet my pillow that night. It was quiet and cold in my little room, and my breath made frost in the night air. To pass the time that lonely night, I would blow out my warm breath, make clouds or chimney smoke, or little frosty balls. Pa taught me how to do that.

Now he was gone and I was so lonely for him. I remember tryin' to count all the nails around the windows. They was cold, all frosted up-like. My countin' wasn't too good yet, but I tried. Still, that snow just kept fallin' out there, down on the cabin. I pulled the quilts up to my chin, all cozy and warm with only my eyes peekin' out. Sleep just wouldn't come.

Next thing I knew, I opened my eyes and it was daylight. Fact was, the sun was shinin'. Shinin'? I scrambled out of my warm bed, shuffled into my overhauls and big sweater. Then I slipped on my thick socks, grabbed my boots and headed for the warm cookstove. I could hear Old Pap and Ma in the kitchen, makin' breakfast sounds and smells. I wanted to be with them in the worst kinda way.

It was a sight to see them there. Pap was a-puttin' wood in the stove, and Ma a-mixin' up biscuits. The coffee was a-bubblin' on the back of the stove. Ma's delicious wild strawberry jam was already a-settin' in the middle of the table.

Her dried flowers that she'd gathered up yesterday from the woods was there on the table. 'Twas always a puzzlement to me how she would pick dead weeds out in the woods. She always thought they was the purtiest wildflowers in the fall and early winter. Never could quite understand that, but it made her happy.

Right beside the jam was a big old slab of butter on a purty little plate. Now, that butter was the best, taken from two or three days' milkin', and churned by my Ma. Those was the days.

"Halloo, Barney Boy!" Old Pap greeted me as I slid into a chair and into my boots.

"Mornin'. Smells good," I said quietly, sorta lookin' down, I guess.

I noticed Ma and Old Pap lookin' at each other. I guess they was more used to me bein' loud and rambunctious, but I didn't feel that way today. My long, lonely night was over. I was grateful that it was day and, but I still felt sad and empty somehow.

106

I tried to smile, really I did. I wondered at Pap when I saw him wink at Ma, sly-like. Then he smiled at me and patted the top of my head. Made me feel warm inside.

Breakfast was good. We had fried eggs, big slices of ham, fresh, hot biscuits with lots of Ma's butter and wild strawberry jam besides. Topped off with hot cocoa made from fresh milk. Pap had already done some of the chores, with the milkin' bein' first ever' day before breakfast.

Soon, we would go out together and fill the wood box from the big stack of dry firewood he kept there, in the lean-to at the back door.

Then we would go out and get eggs, and see to it that all the chickens and livestock had plenty of hay, grain, and fresh water. We got the eggs in twice a day in cold weather so's they wouldn't freeze.

Today, we would have to break ice on the troughs for shore. It had been mighty cold. I was so glad to see the sun sendin' its rays through the window there in the kitchen as I got into my big winter coat. It would still be cold, but the sunshine just made you feel warmer.

It shore was a good thing I hadn't had to start to school. I remember thinkin', one more year yet. I really didn't want to leave Ma and Pap. They needed me. I just knew that they did. I needed them, too, I guess. I don't know as I could of put all that into words right then.

Goin' to do chores with Old Pap would help take the sad feelin's away. I knew that, too, but I didn't put that into words either. I just looked forward to goin' and doin' with him. Just me and him.

Ma was there in her apron. She was busy washin' up breakfast dishes, gettin' stuff out to do her bread-makin' that day. It was just a normal sort of mornin'.

I loved when she made bread. You just can't imagine the delicious smells that swarmed all around the cabin on bread-makin' day. My mouth waters even now, just to think of it.

We filled the wood box from the lean-to just outside the door. Then we got our boots on. We had already fed the stock and broke the ice in the water troughs. I gathered the eggs and had the egg basket on my arm. I was headed back toward the cabin when I first saw it.

There it stood all proud-like with Pa's old red scarf tied around its neck. A big lump come up in my throat and I stood there, frozen-like.

Old Pap come up about then, and reached for the egg basket. He said softly, "Want me to take them eggs inside?"

I didn't even look up at him as I mutely handed the basket up to him. I just couldn't take my eyes off that big, old snowman that had wondrously appeared right there by the cabin overnight. It was a miracle, it shorely was.

It had Pa's old pipe in its mouth and a hunk of charred stove wood for a nose. There was two coals for the eyes. Right there on its head was Pa's old floppy hat. The one he wore chorin' and fishin' and sleepin' in the shade. His very favorite hat.

Finally, I was able to get my feet to move. I stumbled through the deep snow over there. I couldn't believe my two eyes.

First thing was, I looked all around for all the usual signs of tracks and trampled snow. You know how when you make a big mess of tracks in the fresh fallen snow to make a snowman. But there wasn't any tracks!

The snow lay all around the feet up to the knees of that great big snowman. Lay like a baby's blanket; soft and clean and all sparkly there in the mornin' sunshine. Shorely must've snowed in the night. There was snow, right on top of Pa's floppy old hat.

Then I just kept lookin' and lookin' at the sight, walkin' round and 'round in a big circle-like, lookin' way up and up at my wonderful new friend.

I knew he would be there all winter-- that's the way of it. When it gets cold and cold, and then snows and snows, it's cold 'till spring comes back.

By an' by, I stopped and stared up at the face of my giant new friend, and I began to talk to him. I guess it was silly-like, thinkin' back on it now, but it seemed the most natural thing to do at the time.

I guess I stayed out there a long time, pourin' my heart out to that chunk of snow and ice. I was purely feelin' better ever' minute. I kept a-shufflin' my boots in the snow there, and puttin' my hands in and out of my pockets.

I told him how I missed Pa, and how it hurt, and how Ma and me had moved into Pap's cabin now. Then I told him to tell Pa how I missed him. Don't know what made me think he might know Pa, or iffen I really thought that at all, but it felt good just to say the words.

After a good while, I stopped my chatterin' and realized I had already missed the milk separatin' and washin' the eggs, and I better get inside and help out. After all, I was Mama's little man now.

I turned and began to run through the deep snow, best I could, a-stumblin' and rushin' so. My heart was a-poundin' harder than hard!

I was wildly happy and began to laugh, and then I began to cry. As I got to the steps, there stood Old Pap, a-smilin' a crooked little smile with his arm around Ma and her arms held out to me.

I fell into a joyous heap with them. We was a-laughin', a-cryin', and a-talkin' all at once. There I was a-tellin' 'em all about my wonderful snowman out in the yard. I told 'em about how I had me a new friend!

I didn't think of it till later, but Ma had tears on her face, too. That night I wondered about that, as I thanked God for my wonderful new friend.

My little room was cold again and my breath was frosty. There was frost on the nail-heads by the window there, but I was warmer than I had been in months.

I studied about how that snowman had my Pa's hat on his head, and how great it was that Pa's scarf was there, too. Then I remembered my Pa's old worn out pipe a-stickin' out of his mouth-like.

Now, how do you suppose that all got out there on that snowman, and how did that snowman get there in the first place? I began to wonder hard about all that.

After all, the only snowmen I ever saw was when someone worked harder than hard to build one! I had done it many a time with my Pa.

First thing is, you roll up one real giant snowball and put it right where you want the snowman. Did you know that first one's so heavy that you scarcely can even move it into place? Especially when it's a big one like my Manny. Well, it is. I named him that, 'cause he was my big man, my Manny.

Anyway, then you roll up another big snowball. Then another, and you have to gather up stuff to put on the top ball to make it look like a person, like a nose, eyes, and such. Sometimes, on the middle snowball you tie a rope for a belt and push rocks in for buttons. They's lotsa ways to make a snowman into a person.

Well, right there in my warm bed, all of a sudden I *knew* where my Manny had come from. I remembered Old Pap winkin' and smilin' at Ma sly-like that mornin', and my heart surged with joy!

I jumped right up out of that bed in my woolen underwear and dashed out where Mama and Pap was sittin' by the fireplace. They looked surprised when I dived right into Pap's lap and hugged him as hard as I could.

Ma's sewin' got real still in her lap, and he started to laugh. I had finally realized he must have worked a long time in the middle of the night to build Manny.

I just didn't have words to tell him thank you. That snow was so purty-like when I found him, so it musta' snowed after Pap did all that work.

And there was Ma, with tears on her face again, so I went over and gave her a big hug to make her feel better. I still couldn't find words to tell them how wonderful I felt.

Besides, that lump was in my throat again. So, I crawled up in Pap's lap and sat with them a while beside the fire. It was a good, quiet time, with Ma sewin' and smilin', and me and Pap a-rockin'.

Then one day, he called out to me where I was playin' inside the cabin by the fireplace. Ma was busy with something in the kitchen, so I jumped right up and ran to the door. There, a-standin' beautiful as ever, was the horses hitched up to the sleigh!

I let out a whoop and hurried to get my coat and hat on, and noticed Ma was doin' the same. I asked her where we was a-goin', and she gave me that sweet little grin of hers

She didn't say anythin', just handed me a picnic basket. Then, she caught up the bricks off the back of the stove into some big blankets.

I knew it would be a wondrous, long ride in the sleigh. There would be no sleigh bells 'til Christmas, but I knew they would be on the harness by then. Pa had always fetched them from Pap's big barn around Christmas-time.

I tell you, I hardly missed those bells that day, 'cause it was purely glorious glidin' along in that there sleigh.

The wind in my face was cold as ice, but I didn't even care. I just pulled up my scarf over my mouth and nose and yelled to high heaven in joy.

I was purely noisy 'til Ma sorta poked me in the side with her elbow and gave me "that look." Oops! 'Course, you know the one. Every Ma saves that look special-like to tell their young'uns to behave.

She just pulled down her own scarf to do it. I just grinned sheepish-like there behind my scarf. She must've seen it in my eyes, 'cause she grinned right back at me, and then she pulled her scarf back up. But, I didn't holler no more.

It was a wonderful day with that long ride on the sleigh. Then there was the picnic with a campfire to warm us and our foot bricks right up again.

Did you know a picnic tastes best when you eat it beside a campfire and drink hot chocolate 'til it plumb burns your throat? Well it does, and that's the truth of it.

Then the best part was that when we got done with our picnic, we had another long ride on the sleigh. We took a lot of rides that winter, and it was a blessin' to my heart.

Then, a few days after that first ride, as I headed out for chorin', I found a big old pile of snowballs right outside the door! I was walkin' behind Pap, and him a-limpin' along ahead of me, as usual.

Boy, did I let out a big whoop! Then, I snatched one up and slung it right at Pap's back. I still remember the white glob it made on the back of his coat. Then I heard him start to laugh. It was a deep, soft, chuckle at first; then it was a big, loud, happy guffaw. We had us a time that day playin' snowball fight. It was great!

That was the day he taught me to make snow angels. Did you know you can make angels? Well, you can.

He said to stand straight like a tree with my arms out and fall right over backward. Then I was to move my arms up and down as I lay there in the snow. So I did, and then he reached over and took me by the hand. He carefully pulled me up so as not to muss the snow.

Right there, purty as you please, was a snow angel, complete with wings! It purely was the most purty and wondrous thing you ever saw. So we made more of them all over the place. Big ones and small ones, some messy and some neat as a pin. But, there they was big as life.

You should of seen those angels. Pap told me that we all have a guardian angel and I could pretend those angels was all mine. Ever' last one!

I'm goin' to bed now, me and Buster. The fire's banked, and I'm tuckered. But did you know? For years each summer after that, Pa's hat and old red scarf hung on a nail in my room 'til it was time for the first snowman. Then together, me and my Pap would build a brand new Manny.

Then me and Pap would have snowball fights and build snow forts and all. On top of all that, him, me and Ma took lotsa rides in that there sleigh.

Well, I still missed Pa, and at times it was worse than others, but I never had that hurtin' again like I had that one lonesome night.

I come to understand that verse I had read so many times through the years about how weepin' may be all night, but joy comes in the mornin'.

You see, that cold mornin' when I first found my Manny, my joy was back. I decided later that it had somethin' to do with healin'. Whenever I would miss my Pa, it was always more of a lovin' kind of lonely, not the hurtin' kind. And, did you know? There *is* a difference.

8 Old Pap, Lila, and the Little Baby Duck

"Casting all your care upon Him; for He careth for you."
1 Peter 5:7

This mornin', I was watchin' that old, crippled mallard a-scufflin' for feed in the barn. Now, you know a mallard duck has no business bein' up north in the winter, but when they's crippled-like, they can't hardly make that long trip south.

So, this old fella has wintered here with me and my chickens for nigh on to seven or eight winters already.

I first found him down by the river; there he was with his leg and one wing almost pulled off by who-knows-what. I felt so sorry for him as he wailed a weak quack at me whilst me and Doc Willis fixed him up best we could. Doc did the sewin' on that leg and wing. Even though he was up in his seventies by then, his hand was steady as a rock.

Then I took the injured duck home and cared for him. I didn't really have the heart to take care of that crazy old duck because of Isabel.

You see, my Isabel had suddenly passed away only a coupla months before. I had never hurt so much in my life as I had been hurtin' with the loneliness after she died.

It was so sudden-like. Doc said it was a heart attack, and it plumb took me by surprise. Isabel was such a part of me and my life here that I could hardly function at first.

Both Old Pap and Doc Willis kept encouragin' me to look to the Lord and trust Him to see me through.

Old Pap, at ninety-two, was still as strong as ever where the good Lord was concerned. And he shore was dependin' on Him, too, since Isabel had left us. He missed her sorely, and God gave him strength for each day.

He spent many long hours a-readin' his worn old Bible and prayin'. His trusty dog, Happy, would be a-layin' at his feet. And that old dog was purely a comfort to him, too.

Lookin' back now, I don't know how I would of made it without the Lord God, either.

I am so thankful that Old Pap taught me young to cast my cares on the Lord. Knowin' that He, the Almighty, cared for me truly helped heal my heart.

But, I do know exactly what made me take this crippled old duck in. It was all because of Lila and the little baby duck. I knew that for certain.

All those many years ago, when Miz Dolly and her "granchilluns" lived with us, there come a day that Lila Baby wasn't such a baby any more. She was too big to let us call her that mostly. But there was certain times she allowed it, of course.

Lila Baby loved to roam the woods out back; her and her three big sisters. They went all over, but mostly they loved to stay around by the crick for hours and hours, a-lookin' for frogs and crickets and such.

You could be out in the garden, or anywheres, and you would hear them a-squealin' and a-gigglin' to beat the band. It was a sound purely like music to our ears. All of us was delighted when those little colored gals was happy.

Then, one bright summer day, Pap and I was in the garden. We was a-pullin' the first green onions and the last of the early peas when we saw them comin'.

Them little gals was all bunched together, a-walkin' almost like one wide person. Not a sound from any of them, and they had the most solemn little faces. We knew somethin' was bad wrong.

Settin' our baskets down, we hurried toward them. Then I could see Lila's little black face, full of anguish and the tears a-flowin' like a river.

"Lila Baby, what's wrong?" I called as we hurried to them.

"Lila Baby, Sugar, what is it?" Pap almost skipped in his haste to get to the troubled little trio who closely followed their baby sister. He stumbled to his knees as we reached her. Then we could see she had somethin' small cradled in her tiny little hands.

It was almost the same color as her tawny black skin, and at first, we couldn't tell what it was.

"A pore wittle ducky, Pap, a pore wittle ducky," she wailed tragically. With her colorful little pigtails bobbin', she hiccuped between the words and the sobs as she tried to tell us her story. "It almost dwownded, Unca Bawney!" said Lilly May sadly. "It gonna die," she declared knowin'ly.

"Not drownded. Drowned!" corrected Liza Jane, always the little mama to her sisters. It was no wonder that she grew up and had herself a fine husband and a passel of young'uns to mother over. She purely loved to do that even as a little girl.

"That's what she said," Louisa howled. "He almost *drowned!* And he's *not* gonna die, in the name of Jesus!"

She was seven and our little preacher girl. Oh, how she loved goin' to church and the family Bible readin' times we all had together. She loved to hear the promises read from God's book. So, when she grew up, she was the finest, most dedicated little missionary lady you ever saw. She never even married, as she was so busy with her mission work at the orphanage there in China, of all places. I guess them was her own "little chilluns."

But now, the tears began to flow as she considered the possibility that the little duck might not live.

"Okay, okay," Old Pap said gently as he put his arms around Lila's shakin' little shoulders. She was almost four but such a tiny little thing. She was all delicate and dainty-like.

"Let's see what you have there."

Well, the little ducklin' apparently had been separated from his brothers and sisters, and either was starvin' or hurt and not able to swim right. He was exhausted and layin' limp in Lila's little brown hands. His small body heaved as he tried to breathe, and he shivered besides.

"Come on, Lila Baby," I said, as I patted Pap on the shoulder. "Let's get him in by the cookstove and warm him up. Maybe he will feel better after he dries out and gets somethin' to eat."

Pap looked up at me and smiled a thank-you as I helped him to his feet. I carried Lila and the baby duck on one arm, and had a small, black hand wrapped securely in my other hand.

The other two girls took Pap's hands, and we all trooped toward the house, callin' out for Ma, Isabel, and Miz Dolly to get things ready.

The ladies was true to form and took the little crisis seriously. Miz Dolly hurried to make a small bed for the little bird out of an old flannel rag, whilst Ma was quickly warmin' up some milk. And of course, there was Isabel, wipin' tears and comfortin' ever'one at once-like.

Pap gently wiped the fuzzy little body with a dry cloth. Then, Ma got some of the milk down him. I wondered how milk might do on a bird what had never had such before, but I figgered Ma knew. She just plain knew what to do, times like that. I didn't know how, but she knew.

Lookin' back, I can't help but chuckle at how all of us scurried about, carin' for that little baby duck and all the little gals that put so much stock in his well bein'. We was runnin' around like a bunch of little mice.

We must have made quite a sight, a-wipin' noses and helpin' ever'one off with their wet shoes and such-like.

Ma and Miz Dolly was a-droppin' their laundry chores and Isabel was a-shovin' her bread-makin's aside to tend to the situation. I remember she had flour on her purty little nose.

I helped Isabel get some lemonade and cookies ready for the girls, as we knew they would need a treat after all the excitement died off.

We all enjoyed our treats, and after a while, the little duck seemed to be restin' peacefully in his warm little bed by the stove.

We had coaxed the girls up to the table where we all had a snack and a good, long talk about our dilemma. 'Course, we had some of Miz Dolly's buttermilk pie and it went right good after all that hustle and bustle.

Did we take him back and try to find his family? Would they accept him iffen he had been with people?

Pap didn't much think so. And besides, Ma figgered they was already gone by now. She declared that mama ducks don't keep their young'uns in the same place too long. It gets too dangerous.

The girls wanted to know, "Well, what do you feed a baby duck anyway?" Miz Dolly told them that it was the same as chickens-they just eat what their mama eats.

What does she eat? Where do they sleep? How do they keep warm? Can we keep him? Where would he live?

We don't have a mama duck, so how will he know what to eat? The questions come faster than we five adults could answer.

Finally, Pap threw up his hands. "Whoa now," he declared. "One thing at a time!"

He took charge from there, a-makin' the little ones raise their hand to ask a question. Then finally, we had an organized discussion, and ever'one was finally able to eat pie and cookies and drink their lemonade.

Liza Jane even had time to tell Lila Baby to wipe her mouth. Then, Lila boldly announced that she wasn't a baby anymore, and don't call her that. I just shake my head and chuckle at the remembrance. Iffen I'd a-been a fly on the wall that day, I would've seen quite a show!

I'd a-seen that after a while, no one noticed when Lila Baby quietly slipped out of her chair. Then she just slid right down onto the floor beside that sleepin' little duck. She looked so cute there watchin' him with her thumb in her sweet little mouth. Her colorful little piggy tails was a-stickin' out all over the place.

She curled up as close as she could, put her arm around the small flannel rag bed and drew it near to her heart. The next thing any of us knew, there she was a-sleepin' down there on the floor next to her little patient.

Of course, it was decided right then and there that we had to keep the little thing iffen it lived. It would plumb break that little girl's heart iffen we didn't try to give it a home. So, the whole family- all 'ceptin' Lila

Baby who was a-sleepin' on the floor- held hands and prayed for that small little bird.

Old Pap -- bless him -- he prayed fervently, a-tellin' God all about it like a good friend talks to a good friend. He said that the Bible told us that God marks the fall of a sparrow. For shore, we all agreed that He knew all about this tiny little baby duck who needed His help now.

Each little child, and each of us grownups, too, prayed for the duck, and for little Lila Baby, no matter what the Lord's will might be. Those little girls was gettin' a first-hand lesson in a-castin' their cares right on the Lord.

As we sat there, all a-holdin' hands-like, suddenly we heard a funny sound. We all opened our eyes and looked at each other in surprise, and then down at Lila Baby and her ducky.

There they was, a-lookin' at each other, and that little bird was quackin'! Softly at first, then a loud protest. We watched as it shuffled closer to Lila and snuggled up against her as she lay there smilin'.

"Praise God!" It was Pap who shouted first. Then we all started in, and Ma and Miz Dolly shushed us so's we wouldn't scare the life right outa the little thing.

I smile now ever' time I think of that day, and I think of it just about ever' time I go out and feed my crippled old duck in the barn. I also smile as I recall how his comin' brought Lila's baby duck story back to me, and how my crippled old duck helped ease my pain after losin' my Isabel so recently.

It still makes me smile to remember that the Lord does indeed mark the fall of a sparrow, and He does care about the broken heart of a grievin' husband. He is just always there- sometimes in the needs of an injured baby bird.

I remember many times lookin' out over the yard and the field south of the house there where Lila and Lucy would be playin'. She named the duck "Lucy," of all things. She said it had to be an "L" name because all the girls had "L" names!

There she would be hoppin' along and that little duck a-waddlin' right behind her. They was shore attached, Lila and her little baby duck. She took responsibility for her ducky, too.

We learn't later on that the ducky really was a girl, by the way. She lived a number of years and gave us more little mallard ducks that flew south come fall.

Her mate moved right in and never flew south again, or maybe he never had. He became part of the family, too, only he kept his distance 'cept where Lucy was concerned.

Did you know that mallard ducks are mates for life? Well, they are. It is a wondrous thing to see as they raise their little families together.

Lucy never did fly south, either. Maybe she didn't want to leave her mate, or maybe she thought it might break Lila's little heart. Maybe that little duck thought she was a chicken, and chickens don't even fly south! That just might be the truth, too, because we had a mother hen who was a-hatchin' chicks, about the time Lucy come along. Pap put her there with the little chicks and she fit right in.

She followed the mother hen around and ate what she ate, but she quacked instead of chirpin'. That always made us laugh. Also, she looked different with her little webbed feet.

She just never did get the hang of scratchin' with the chickens, but she soon learn't to follow the others and help them eat whatever they scratched up.

At night, she went into the chicken house and roosted on a low ledge in the hay that Pap built just for her. That is, after she was old enough to not be in under her foster mama's feathers at night.

Later on, her mate, Lavern, joined her there on her roost. Of course, his name had to be an "L" name, too!

When she was still small, Lila Baby took Lucy out often and let her swim in an old, steel dishpan that Ma gave her.

When Lucy was bigger, they would go out by the crick together. Pap and Lila would help her find worms and crickets, and Lucy had lots of good meals out there, too. Lucy had become Lila's constant playmate. For several years, Lucy was her favorite personal pet.

Lila mothered over all the nests of eggs and little ducklin's over the years, and I fully believe that is why when Lila grew up, she decided to go off to school to become a vet'narian. We was all so proud of her and her little baby duck.

And, maybe that's why I named my old crippled duck Lucky. 'Twasn't really luck that brought him to me, or luck that brought little Lucy into our lives, or luck that brought Miz Dolly and her grandchilluns to us. But, do you know what? Sometimes, I have felt just plain lucky. And, to me, that is just another word for blessed!

9 Old Pap, Hannah, and the Teacher

"...lo, I am with you alway,
even unto the end of the world. Amen."
Matthew 28:20b

Today was the first day of school. Whilst I had my second cup of coffee out on the big, wide, front porch enjoyin' the smells of a misty mornin', I saw the school bus go by. Now, *that* brought such a rush of memories of my childhood, of Miz Dolly's little ones startin' their little school in the back room with Isabel.

I had memories of all the little nieces and nephews goin' off to school each fall, and just more memories than I could try to count.

But, the one that seemed to stay with me all day as I went about my business was the memory of my own self, and when I started off to school for the first time.

The summer before I started to school was so hard on me. I was happy, and then I was a-scar't. I was all growed up-like, and then I never wanted to grow up. I was excited, and then I was afraid.

I would go to bed at night, ready to wake up and have the first day of school. Then, I would wake up full of relief that it wasn't. It was a miserable, terrible time for a six-year-old!

I guess I would say that Pap helped me the most in gettin' through that summer. Of course, then I would talk to Ma and verify his stories, and that helped, too.

The first time I cried on his shoulder, we was sittin' on a pole fence back of the pasture. It was springtime and a nice sunshiny day, too. It was a good piece 'til time for school to even start.

Don't really know what got me thinkin' about it, but I knew that before snow would fly again, I would be goin' to school ever' day. Ever' day for the rest of my life, it seemed.

The mare had a new foal, and we should'a been havin' a good time watchin' her play. She hopped all stiff-legged and romped around like the little filly she was.

Only trouble was, I just couldn't keep my mind off the fact that I was gonna have to go to school come fall. I wouldn't even get to watch her that much when school started, and I wouldn't even have time to sit on the fence with my best friend, Pap.

I just sat there, quiet-like, with my chin in my hands and my elbows on my knees. Didn't take my Pap long to figger out somethin' wasn't right with me, 'cause usually I kept his ears busy a-listenin' with all my chatter, and right now they was gettin' quite a rest. He always noticed when I was quiet-like.

Pap had a way with young'uns, a-gettin' them to talk-like. You hardly ever knew he really wanted you to tell him all about it, but he just knew how. So, shore as the world, it wasn't long 'til I was a-pourin' out my heart to him.

With my fists clenched tightly, I told him how I felt, an' that I just couldn't stand the idea of goin' off to school thataway. How I would miss him and Ma so much. Before I was done, the tears was splashin' down the front of my shirt right onto my dungarees.

Pap's arm felt mighty good when it slid across my shoulders-like, and I never did understand why that made me cry all the harder. I just sobbed and sobbed. Soon, he had me up in his arms and we had slid down into the grass there along the fence line, me a-cryin' and him a-rockin' me back and forth.

He said things like how he understood, how he had went through the same thing, and how he remembered holdin' my own Ma the very same way. How it wasn't unusual at all for me to be feelin' that way.

He said how he loved me and how God loved me. He told me how God would be with me at school, too, just like He always is at home.

Do you know that God is with you all the time? Well, He is.

But that day, I hadn't never thought of that before, so that's when I pushed back and looked up into his face. I remember he was smilin' his gentlest, very best "I love you" smile. It purely warmed my heart.

And he kept on smilin' when I asked was that really true that God would be right there with me even in school? Was that really true?

He began noddin' his head when I started to talk. Along with a good, long hug, he assured me that yes, it was true that I didn't really have to go to school alone at all. He said that I was *never* goin' to be alone!

Pap told me how Jesus had said right in the Bible that He would be with me always… Jesus would be with me the whole time!

Well, that shed a whole new light on things, and I sniffed real hard and wiped my face on my shirttail. Pap handed me his big red handkerchief. Then I blew my nose good and proper-like.

Then, I sighed real deep-like, and just curled up against Pap where I could hear his heart beatin' behind his flannel shirt. There was no place I would rather be right then.

He had started to talk, and I could tell it was gonna be a good, long story. So's I just settled in and watched the fuzzies blowin' off the dandelions along the fence there.

He chuckled when he was tellin' about Ma and how she was so scar't to go to school the first time, too.

He said one day that summer, her little pigtails flew out behind her as she ran like the wind into the barn. She was so scar't, he told me, that she said she was goin' there to stay so that she would never, never have to go to school.

She said that she would just live there with the barn cats, and she wouldn't need to go away. She wouldn't be in anyone's way and could just drink milk with the cats, so they wouldn't even have to worry about feedin' her.

He said she went on and on tryin' to convince him that she really didn't need to go to school at all. Ever!

Finally, I asked him from my quiet snuggly place in his lap, "Did she ever to go school after all?" Then, he laughed outright. I looked up then, and couldn't help a little smile when I saw his eyes all lit up and twinklin'-like.

"Well, did she?" I seriously wanted to know.

"Of course she did, Barney Boy," he said with a chuckle and a squeeze. He often called me that. It was like his pet name for me, I guess. Even when I was gettin' on up in years and my own hair was greyin', he would call me Barney Boy.

Anyways, that was the day he started tellin' me stories about when Ma first went to school. It was nigh on to 1870 when she started goin'. It was a new adventure almost ever' day.

He said how she was so thrilled the one day when she come home and said she got to help the new teacher fill the lamps, clean chimneys, and trim wicks. Now, that was a dirty, smudgy job, but she was so happy to be workin' with her teacher that she didn't even care she come home with soot on her nose and halfway up her arms.

So, I was beginnin' to figger that goin' to school might not be all bad iffen you could have fun that way. What I couldn't figger was why on earth Ma thought it was fun to clean nasty, dirty oil lamps! But, she did, and that made her happy, so the hearin' of it did make me feel a little better.

But how did she make out the *first* day of school, I wanted to know. Oh, he laughed again as he told me about how at first she was makin'-like she was too sick to get out of bed. Then he told how they finally got her up and she couldn't eat breakfast for bein' so nervous-like.

He said she fidgeted and squirmed whilst Gram, Pap's mama, fixed her hair. Gram even let her wear her favorite Sunday ribbons just for the first day of school to make it special-like.

But when it was time to start out for the one room schoolhouse, they couldn't find her anywhere.

Her older brothers, Harry and Hank, was lookin' ever'where, callin' out, "Hannah! Hannah! You are gonna make us late!"

They didn't want to be late. First of all, 'twas because they had heard there was to be a new teacher, and they was excited about that. They also liked school with all the other young'uns to play with.

Besides, they was learnin' to read, and they shorely did like that. They thought they was plumb growed up, and she was only a baby. They even wanted to know why didn't Pap and Gram just skip it and let her stay home? "After all, Papa," they said, "she is too young to go to school anyhow."

Of course, Pap and Gram didn't agree with that, and they all kept lookin'. They eventually found her a-hidin' up in the haymow with hay a-stickin' out all over her head, and tears runnin' down her face.

"Please, Pappy," she cried. "I don't wanna go to school."

But, they finally all trooped off to school, the boys leadin' the way and Pap carryin' my Ma- little Hannah- in his arms.

Gram walked along beside him carryin' Ma's lunch pail and tellin' her all about her very own first day of school. She told how she was a-scar't, too, and how it all turned out to be for nothin'. That was because she loved school just like Hank and Harry did.

Fact was, Gram told her about when Hannah's own Pappy was a young'un and his very first day of school came. She told about how he had come home so happy that day because teacher had let him help stack firewood in the wood box. He was so glad how his little desk was right next to the stove, and he would be warm as toast all winter.

That made my Ma smile and she gave her Pappy a squeeze around his neck as they walked along there.

Well, what happened when she *got to school,* I wanted to know. That was the part that was the scariest for me. Pap chuckled and moved me to his other leg, sayin' that leg was goin' to sleep. We got readjusted there on the grass.

By then, I was more interested, so I sat up straight and watched his face as he talked about my Ma's first day at school. I needed to know what happened. I just needed to know in the worst way.

"Well," he said, "when we got there, there was lots of other little children, all ages, and they was outside the school-house runnin' and playin'. They was jumpin' rope, and throwin' balls, and yellin', you know."

Then he told how when Ma saw it, her eyes got real big and she said, "Oh, that's the church! Are we goin' to church, Pappy? I thought we was goin' to school!"

Now my Pap laughed outright as he remembered her puzzlement, as she hadn't realized that school was right inside the church-house.

Well, that was no surprise to me, I said; I knew that already because we had went to the Christmas play that the school had, and it was right in the church-house.

Besides, some of the cousins had told me that the church *was* the school-house.

Well, that seemed so strange to me because I couldn't figger that. How could a church be a school-house and a school could be a church-house? I think that Pap knew I was comin' 'round because I had started to chatter again.

He told me that as soon as Ma saw that the school was right in the church-house, her fear left her. She declared right then that she knew Jesus would be there with her, especially right in church, even iffen it was school.

She scrambled to get down and join her little friends from Sunday school and forgot to even say goodbye!

Eight year old Harry come back a shakin' his head and got her lunch bucket. He gave his Papa and Gram a hug, explainin' all growed up-like that Hannah and Hank was just too excited to remember.

Then Pap gave me a good, long hug, and we got up and started for the house. I couldn't believe when he said it was most time for lunch already, and Ma would be waitin' for us. We hadn't even started weedin' the new spring garden.

I felt so much better, though, that I even skipped as we walked along together. He held my hand in his big strong one.

There was many more talks that summer as my concerns would get the best of me, and I would quiz Pap some more about when Ma went to school.

But the very best story was the one where he said that Ma made a new friend in school that first year. His name was Timmy. Yes, the little boy that lived up the road. He was the new teacher's very own son, and one day, many years later, Ma married him and he was my own Pa.

Now, that made Ma's first teacher a very special person in my eyes, because that made him my other Grandpa! He had died before Ma and Pa married, but it made him so real to me and so very special.

So, ever' time I would get really scar't about school, I would think that maybe my teacher would be part of my family someday, too. Then I'd feel a right-smart better.

Sometimes, I laugh when I think about how scar't I was to start to school. We didn't even have a school bus way back then, like the one I saw today. As it turned out, though, my first teacher was never related to me.

Ever'thin' changed, though, when I learn't that my teacher loved the Lord the same way my family did. That took away all the fears I had that long summer before school started.

Not ever' teacher I had was a believer, but the first one was, and that got me off to a right good start! I do remember a-prayin' for those other teachers to make Jesus Christ their very own Savior.

It's gettin' dark now, and all the chores are done, so me and Buster are headin' in for the night. I am gonna have me some wild grape jam on my fresh bread.

I still chuckle when I remember Old Pap goin' down to old Elmer Frackley's farm. Happy Hopscotch would be a-taggin' along, like he always did, of course.

He'd go out behind that big old silo there and pick wild grapes for jam. I still go there, and I make it myself now, from Old Pap's recipe collection. He got that recipe right from Miss Bethany. Fact is, today I made bread from his own bread recipe he had there.

I think I will have a good, long talk with God about how thankful I am for Old Pap, and that God was with me in school. Fact is, that He has been with me ever' day before and since. He has been with me for my whole entire life, as a matter of fact.

Then, I think I will tell Him how thankful I was for my first school teacher. Next, I will thank Him for Ma, and her first school teacher, who turned out to be my very own grandpa. Do you know? It just don't get no better than that.

10 Old Pap, Me, and Huck Finn

"Trust in the Lord with all thine heart;
and lean not unto thine own understanding."
Proverbs 3:5

Buster was sittin' there this afternoon whilst I puttered around in the cemetery on the hill overlookin' the river. I was a-trimmin' grass, a-pullin' weeds, and a-rakin' the first of the fall leaves away. He was watchin' the old river goin' by just like he usually does, when suddenly he barked. Not a big loud one, but just a gruff "hello" kind of bark. About that same time, I heard familiar shouts. Brought a big smile to my face. It purely did!

"Hi, Uncle Barney! Uncle Barney!"

Well, there Glennie and Scott was, on a raft, mind you! Those little boy, map-drawin' cousins, was a-floatin' down the river on a raft. Oh, did that take me back. I hollered a big halloo and waved big.

It took a time for them to get outa sight 'round the bend in the river. We waved and shouted and celebrated the seein' of one another 'til they was gone, me a-chucklin' the whole while.

There was a big ole' red ant bed there by the old stone bench when I sat down. It had to be a new one, 'cause 'twasn't there last time I sat there. I watched them goin' under the little picket fence as my mind went back.

I well remember readin' about Tom Sawyer, and his buddy, Huckleberry Finn, when I was a young'un in school. There was a lot about things 'way back then that I didn't understand about slavery, and seein' who could be the baddest boy, and all that. One thing I did understand was that I wanted a river raft in the worst way.

Sittin' there a-watchin' the ants scurryin' around this mornin', it all come back like a flood.

I had been a-dreamin' of it for days whilst the teacher took several weeks in the readin' of those adventures of Huck and his buddy, Tom Sawyer.

In bed at night I would imagine the thrill it would be to lay smack-dab in the middle of a log raft with a twig a-stickin' outa my mouth and a lunch all tied up beside me in my Pa's big red bandana.

I would lay there and watch the sky. The clouds and the branches goin' by above me, and there would be birds come and land on my knees there where I had them bent up toward the sky.

By 'n by, I would get my fishin' pole and fish for a while, and later I would take a swim. Maybe I would wear my short pants, and maybe I would just wear nothin' at all. Ahh, the dreamin' of it was most pleasurable.

Then, the one day come when I dashed home from school with my mind made up. I knew just who to ask about buildin' me a river raft. I knew Pap would help me. I just knew it! He was a builder after all, and he could build anything!

It was springtime and the river was thawed out, but cold as icicles. I didn't care.

What I had to have was a raft to put on that river, and me on that raft.

Pap wasn't to home when I got there, bein' off in the woods, a-cuttin' firewood. My hopes about dashed my heart into bits when Ma said she didn't think that her Pappy would have time for such as that. He had too much other work to get done.

He had so much spring work with summer crops and gardenin' comin' up, besides all his other odd jobs to get done. She first said not to bother him about it, and I thought I would just die, right then and there.

Then she got a strange, little smile playin' around her mouth. She said, alright, that I could ask my Pap, but not to be disappointed iffen he said no.

No? There was just no way he would say no! "Please, God, please don't let him say no," I prayed. For a minute there, I had to really get serious and tell God that iffen he did say no, I would understand and wait 'til we could do it. Maybe later in the summer.

But in my heart of hearts, I really wanted that river raft. I had already waited so

long. At least, it seemed that way to me, bein'
I was only nine or ten years old at the time!
So, with all my fingers and toes crossed, off I
went to find Pap.

Now I 'bout ran in circles at first tryin'
to decide which way to go to find him in the
woods. I ran this a-way and that a-way just
tryin' to figger out which way he was. Once I
finally got him spotted, it didn't take long to
get there and I skidded right up to him there
in the shade of the big, old pine trees.

"Whoa there, boy! What's the big
hurry?" he wanted to know.

Then, I was a-talkin' so fast a-tellin'
him all my plans and how to build a raft and
such-like. Finally, he held his hand up for me
to wait.

Then, he took his big, old red bandana,
wiped his face, and sat right down on a stump
there where he had just cut down a tree. He
said for me to just hold onto my britches and
get my breath. Then he bade that we would
have to think on it for a while. Oh, I thought
I might just get sick iffen he said we couldn't
build my river raft. I was that set on it.

He just sat there. It seemed like forever. Pap was a-gazin' off in the trees there, a-thinkin'-like. Iffen I'd start to say somethin', he would put his finger over his lips to shush me. I had the awfullest time keepin' my thoughts to myself.

Do you know it can be hard to keep your mouth shut sometimes? Well, I tell you, it shore can!

It seemed like he studied on it forever, when at long last, he turned and looked me right in my own two eyes. Do you know what he said?

"Barney Boy, I think that is a right good idea. I got it all figgered out, and here is what we are gonna do. Now, I will explain it all to ya, boy!"

I tell you, joy just about took the top of my head off as I stared straight at his face whilst he gave his plan right out, step by step.

Well, 'twasn't long 'til that river raft dream become the real thing. I couldn't believe my own two eyes when I stood there beside that flowin' river, and there sat my very own river raft. Well, me and Pap's, that is, for he purely designed it and mostly it was all put together.

Trouble was, he had to go off with one of his old friends who had come a-visitin', and there I stood with my mostly finished river raft. But I was makin' me a plan, for shore.

He had made the logs flat on one side so's they pushed right up against one 'nuther. And it was right there, just waitin' to be lashed together.

Pap had said it takes special knots to hold such a thing, but, as I studied on it, with the ropes right in my hands, I had it figured out. I could do this. "Yes, I can do this!" I said to those logs a-sittin' there.

So, before long, I had twined, twisted, and tied them ropes 'til my raft was ready to go- or so I thought.

I was purely excited to get it into the water to try it out. I knew Pap and his buddy would be a-crossin' the river bridge before long as they should be back soon. I purely wanted to be a-floatin' along toward that bridge when he got there. He would be so surprised! So, I heaved, and shoved, and grunted, and 'twasn't long till I had it half-way in the water.

Then I remembered my Papa's red handkerchief. I was hungry anyhow, so's I scurried back to the cabin and quick wrapped up some of Ma's biscuits, and took off back to the river.

I could see her back there in the garden, and I waved a big old wave as I took off.

I plumb skidded down the bank there, tossed my bundle onto the raft and pushed that raft right into the water as I jumped into the smack-dab middle of it.

"Yeehawww!!!" I yelled so loud I just knew Ma would hear me and come to see. But as I got to that first bend in the river, she still hadn't come into view, so's I figured she'd see it later. I was disappointed, though. I was that proud of that raft.

Now, mind you, I never thought it through just how I was a-gonna get back. Of course, Pap had been a-whittlin' a coupla long pushin' poles, but they was a-layin' on the bank back there.

I never even thought about that, though, as I sat with my knees up and a-floatin' down my favorite river. I thought my heart would plumb bust out with joy, I was that happy. I just laid right back and peered up at the trees a-floatin' by.

Well, of course, I was the one a-floatin' along, peaceful-like. That is, right up 'til the big bump what just about tossed me off! Iffen Pap hadn't of put those handholds on that last log, I woulda fell right off!

I had crashed right into Table Rock! Of all things! When I sat up, there it was, bigger than life! The river was slowly a-pushin' me around it. So's, I just held on 'til things settled down.

Only trouble was, they didn't. That was just the beginnin' of my troubles. 'Twasn't long 'til a log slipped loose and I was a-scramblin' to try and get it tied up again.

The other trouble was that whilst I was a-tyin' that side, the log on the other side come a-loose.

Before long, I was a-cryin' and my nose was a-runnin' so bad it plumb dripped down whilst I was frantically tryin' to get things to hold together.

First one, then another log slipped a-loose and I just wasn't gettin' any of it to hold. My Papa's handkerchief, which was full of wet biscuits, slung from side to side as I worked.

First thing I'd done was push my fist right through the loose knot in the middle of that bundle so I wouldn't lose Papa's handkerchief or my biscuits! But now, I wasn't thinkin' on that at all.

The water was so cold, it plumb made me shiver, so my words was right shaky.

"Dear God," I sobbed, "I'm sorry I didn't wait for Pap. Please don't let me die out here on this river!"

I was so scar't that I never thought it through. I could swim and just let that old raft go. But, I just kept a-workin', and a-cryin', and seein' those logs get away, one by one.

I had the last two logs between my knees, a-bawlin' my eyes out, with my face down on them wet logs.

"Barney! Barney Boy! Get off, Barney! Just get off!"

Finally, I heard my Pap's wonderful voice through my own racket. He was a-tellin' me to just get off and stand up. When I looked up, there he was a-standin' on the old river bridge with his buddy, and they was a-laughin'! Laughin', mind ya!

Suddenly, I realized I was plumb over at the edge of that there river, so's all I had to do was stand up and I was saved! I plumb couldn't believe my own two eyes.

Oh, how I did whoop and holler then, thankin' God and my Pap with all my heart. Then I was a-laughin' right along with the men there on that bridge!

It was later in his arms that I got all embarrassed-like as he reminded me that the Lord was with me that whole time. He told me how we can trust Him to take care of us even when we make mistakes.

By then, I felt really bad because I knew I shouldn't of done that raft without Pap. I truly learn't my lesson though, about how I can trust God all the time.

Then he said we could get that river raft back together. But by then, you know what? I didn't really care no more, and you know what else? Even though I knew God had been with me on that there river, I didn't wanna be Huck Finn no more. Fact was, I never ever wanted a river raft again after that! And that's the truth!

11 Old Pap and Roscoe

*"I have compassion on the multitude,
because they have now been with me three days,
and have nothing to eat:"*
Mark 8:2

It downright made me laugh today when I thought about Roscoe. I was uptown to have pie with the fellas when I saw a pickup truck with a big old... Well, I won't tell you just yet what it was that reminded me. There'll be plenty of time for that later.

Thing was, it come back so clear. As I sit now, thinkin' on it, it's clear as a bell. We was a-sittin' in front of the fireplace on a cold winter's night when Old Pap was near ninety. Me and him and dear Isabel. It was a quiet, peaceful evenin' long after supper time.

I remember how Isabel was a-sittin' and a-rockin' and her knittin' needles was a-clickin' along at a right-smart pace. She was busy there as we relaxed.

Old Pap was leanin' back in the easy chair sorta day-dreamin' into the fire that was a-cracklin' there. Happy was a sittin' at his feet, his little tail a-waggin' just a bit.

Me, I had just about finished the weekly newsaper that we'd had around a few days already. Never can seem to get them read right off.

Anyhow, I remember how Isabel's rocker slowed a mite, and her knittin' needles did, too, like they sometimes did when she was gonna say somethin'. I shore do miss hearin' her needles that way. Fact is, sometimes I miss her somethin' awful.

But that evenin', she slows down and I looks up over my readin' glasses. Just as I thought, she looked right at Old Pap.

Then she smiles and says, "Pap, tell us about Roscoe."

It was sorta like a question and sorta like a request. The truth was, I knew for shore that she already knew all there was to know about Roscoe.

Another truth was that she just purely loved the hearin' of that old, old story of

Pap's. I raised my eyebrows up like I always did.

You oughta' seen him that night. He cleared his throat, sat straight up in the old easy chair, and smiled ear-to-ear-like. He was at his best a-tellin' a story.

Happy, that silly old dog, jumped right up to his feet. Then he stood there a minute starin' up at Old Pap and a-waggin' his little black tail real big.

Soon, though, he turned in a circle and lay back down. T'wasn't long 'til he figgered out Old Pap wasn't a-goin' nowhere. I just smiled.

Old Pap, he loved the story as much as Isabel did, and all the family had always loved to hear about Roscoe.

I do 'specially remember that night because Old Pap had aged so much by then. When he smiled like that, the blue veins up beside his temples was plain to see.

He was slight built to begin with, and by then, he was plumb skinny. His skin was thin and sweet lookin', as Isabel often said when he would complain about his "old man's hands." She always had a way of makin' good out of just about anythin'.

"Well," he says, "after you went and made my favorite dessert for supper and all, I guess I could talk about the good old days. Shore, I'll tell you about Roscoe!"

He chuckled and smiled some more and began to talk. "It was 'long about 1844," he said with a far-away kind of smile.

She stopped her knittin' for a spell and watched his face, all lit up-like with that twinklin' smile of his. I just laid the newspaper aside and settled in for a nice long story. It would be better than anythin' in that paper anyway.

I also knew it would be more interestin' than anythin' on the radio there, and that was what I had been thinkin' on listenin' to.

Even iffen I'd already heard this story a hunderd times or more, it was always good to hear. Fact was, I had heard it since I was knee-high to a grasshopper.

It all began when Old Pap was only knee-high his own self. He liked to say it was his first lesson in compassion. His grandpa later told him that he had felt compassion just like Jesus had, and that was why the experience had touched his little heart so strong-like.

Pap was just a small little fella when Roscoe come into his life. He says he was in between a small tot and a schoolboy when it happened. He must've been only about four years old.

He told us that him and his grandpa had been up to the livery stable in town. They were goin' to get some horseshoes for their old mule. Him and his ma and pa lived right there at grandpa's farm, he said. He purely loved goin' places with his grandpa.

Old Pap- or Hal, as he was called in those days- that's short for Harold, you know, was a-pokin' around in the barn there. He was a-lookin' for kittens and such-like. Suddenly, he heard a squealin' sound over in the back stall of the livery barn.

He couldn't figger for the life of him what that sound could be. So, he peeked over his shoulder to make shore no one saw him. Then he snuck back there to have a look-see.

Now, he knew his grandpa didn't like for him to be sneaky, but he just couldn't help hisself, Old Pap told us. That squealin' was the strangest sound he'd ever heard, and he was just beside hisself with curiosity.

He said he jumped when his grandpa called out to him, "Hal! Whatcha doin' back there?" And he told him, "Nothin' much, Pap. I'm just a-lookin' around." So, his grandpa says, "You be careful, and don't get up under those horses' feet, ya hear?!"

He truthfully told him "Yes sir!" He had no intentions of goin' anywheres near those borin' old horses when he could hear somethin' back there that he had never heard before.

'Bout then, he said he started to tippy-toe so's whatever was back there wouldn't know he was a-comin'.

When he got to the last stall, he saw right off that the gate was shut tighter than tight.

He tried, but he couldn't budge it. The fact was, he couldn't even reach the latch, and he wanted to see inside in the worst way.

So, he went around to the side of that last stall. Then he looked in to see was there a horse or such-like in there. It was empty!

Boy, was he happy, Old Pap said. He slipped right on into that stall, lookin' over his shoulder-like. Then, he sidled up to the fence between the two stalls, so that he could look through the slats. What do you think he saw there?

It was a huge mama pig with what seemed like a hunderd little piggies all around her. She was a-lyin' on her side, and they was a-climbin' all over theyselves and all over each other a-tryin' to find theyselves a faucet.

Isabel always smiled at this part, and Old Pap looked up from starin' into the fireplace to see her grin. He grinned back, big as he always did, and went on with his story.

He admitted that there likely wasn't no hunderd piggies in that there pen, but that to him, it shore seemed that-a-way. He stood there for the longest time with his fingers hooked over the rough boards of the stall.

He tried not to move nothin' but his eyeballs 'cause he didn't want to scare them all, not even when he got the awfullest itch behind his knee. He knew enough from wild mama cats that you don't disturb them when they's a-feedin' their little ones.

After a bit, he noticed that the squealin' had stopped. He'd watched long enough that he was wonderin' about all that racket he had heard before. Then, all of a sudden, he heard it again.

"One lonely squeal, the saddest thing I ever heard," Pap said, a-shakin' his small white head back and forth.

About then, Isabel got a sad look and a little pout on her purty lips. I always enjoyed her reaction to Old Pap's stories. Made me smile deep down inside-like.

Somehow, the squealin' wasn't as loud and insistent as it had been before, and little Hal figgered he was just tuckered out from a-squealin' and all. He stood there, transfixed-like, a-watchin' the tiny pink and black form there on the hay.

After a bit, the little baby tried to push his way in up amongst all the rest, so's he could have him some supper, too. The others just pushed all the harder and he was just plain left out. There wasn't even enough faucets for him to even eat.

And that's when Pap got mad, he said. To think, that tiny little baby, and no one would even let him eat, and no one even seemed to care.

Worst of all, even that baby's own mama didn't seem to notice. She just laid there happy as could be with all those little ones a-tuggin' at her and her tail a-swishin' back and forth.

Do you know that you can tell when a critter is happy? His tail is a happy indicator. Well, you can. Just watch his tail!

"Hey!" he shouted suddenly. "Let that little guy in. He's hungry!"

Well, that did it, right then! Mama Pig jumped about a foot off the floor, and little piggies flew ever'wheres, Pap said.

He didn't care; he was that mad. He proceeded to bawl out that whole bunch of selfish pigs, the big one and all the little ones alike.

He told them that God didn't intend for that little one to be hungry and that they'd better make room for him. They could take turns-like, and then ever'one could eat and no one would be hungry.

He was stompin' his little feet there in the soft, mushy hay in the horse stall and the tears was a-fallin' right down his face. He said he didn't know it at the time, but his grandpa had told him all about it later.

Of course, all the commotion brought his grandpa and the blacksmith runnin' to the rear-end of the barn to see what was happenin'.

When they heard his little speech and saw his anger, they couldn't help but laugh. Old Pap said he purely didn't know what was so funny, and he started to cry even harder.

"I was a-wailin' and carryin' on," he solemnly declared. Only there was a twinkle there in his eyes.

171

"Oh, Hal, it's alright. Don't ya fret none." The blacksmith put a work-worn hand on the small boy's shoulder and patted him awkwardly.

"It's just the runt. 'Most always there is one, and they usually die. It's no big deal, happens all the time," the kindly man told him." The strongest will live, and that little rascal just isn't strong enough to push his way in to eat."

"It's no fair!" Pap said he shouted up at the big man. "It's no fair that you would just let Roscoe die like that! He's just a little bitty baby! God wouldn't like that one bit!"

Sobbin', he hugged his grandpa's legs and hid his face. Pap said he thought his heart would break right in two.

He was vaguely aware of the men talkin' quietly to one another. As he cried, he told God how sorry he was that the little piggy would die. He said that he knew God even cared about a tiny sparrow, and so he knew that God cared about little Roscoe. He said "Please, please God, don't let him die! Please, please God, save little Roscoe!"

Next thing he knew, his grandpa was kneelin' down right in front of him wipin' his face and nose with his big, old, red handkerchief. "Here, Hal, you blow now. It's a-gonna be alright," his grandpa said kindly.

Only Pap knew nothin' would be alright iffen Roscoe was left to die that a-way. He shook his head as he blew his nose, and hiccupin' between words, he said so. He was plumb broken hearted, that was what he was.

"Now, ease off, Hal. Listen to what Smithy here said. He said we could take the little fella home with us."

Then that big blacksmith bent down to little Hal and said kindly, "Would you like that, boy?"

"Would I?" Old Pap said he plumb near knocked his grandpa over when he grabbed him around the neck and started to laugh and laugh.

He was happier than happy. Then he rushed to Smithy and hugged his legs, a-thankin' him from the bottom of his heart for savin' that baby. Then, he felt real sorry for shoutin' and bein' rude-like. He was taught to never be rude and to respect his elders, and he said as much to Smithy.

"And, Mr. Smithy, I shore do thank you and thank you for savin' little Roscoe," he said. He purely meant ever' word, too.

Smithy pushed him back and said, "Roscoe?"

"Yes, Roscoe! You said little Roscoe just wasn't strong enough to eat, but he can eat just fine iffen we take him home with us, can't he?"

Little Hal hiccupped real big and said, "We can make shore Roscoe can eat all he wants, and no one will push him away. Right, Grandpa?"

Old Pap always chuckled at this part, because he said his grandpa told him something when he was older. He told him that what Smithy had really said was that "the little rascal" wasn't strong enough to eat. Old Pap said that he thought he said "little Roscoe." Well, by that time, Roscoe had his name, and they would never have changed it.

Suddenly, Pap rushed over to the slatted fence and squatted down low so he could see in more at the piggies' level. There they was, all settled in, a-tuggin' on their mama, and she was as happy as before.

He'd hoped to see Roscoe up there with the others, but there he was, all alone in the hay, lookin' sad and hungry. He said he was the most lonesomest little piggy he ever saw.

Pap told how he'd looked up to see Smithy and his grandpa watchin' him. He asked could they please get Roscoe outta there so's they could take him home and feed him?

Old Pap spoke in a high-pitched little voice and said, "He is plumb starvin' to death." He looked right at Isabel, for he purely did love to see her smile at his story.

At the time, he still didn't know what made Smithy and his grandpa smile right then. The truth was that he was very happy to see Smithy go around to the gate and quietly open it up.

Roscoe was there, right inside the gate. Smithy reached inside and scooped him up quick as a flash, without even disturbin' all the other little piggies.

And, wonder of wonders, he come right over and put the little fella right into Pap's arms.

He said that was the un-snuggliest little animal he ever had held! The little body was firm, scratchy, and warm. It was a good thing he was warm. Even a young'un knew iffen a little baby was cold, that was a bad thing.

Did you know that it's not a good thing for a baby to be cold? Well it's not!

He put that baby pig right inside his shirt then, and boy, did that scratch his bare skin! But, he wanted to make shore little Roscoe stayed warm, and that was that.

You must have figgered out by now that it was a big, old, black pig in a pickup that made me think of Roscoe today. But especially it made me think of Old Pap and his wonderful Roscoe story.

Roscoe lived there on my Old Pap's grandpa's farm for a good many years and was daddy to lots of little babies his own self. But the best part about Roscoe was how he loved Old Pap. They grew up together, you might say.

He always said he guessed Roscoe loved him because he had prayed for the little runt, and because God had saved him, just like that!

12 Old Pap, Me, and the Swingin' Tree

*"And out of the ground made the Lord God to grow ...
the tree of life also in the midst of the garden..." Genesis 2:9a,c*

I sat awhile on the old swing at the swingin' tree today. Well, that swing isn't really old, but the tree is. There has been a long, rope swing there as far back as I can remember.

As the years have rolled by, Old Pap, and then I always made shore the ropes was strong and tight. Then we was careful to see that they was replaced ever' three or four years so that any child, or grownup for that matter, could swing safely.

The ground underneath is worn from many hunderds of pushin' and draggin' feet. There is a deep hollow there to show all the many good times that have been had in the old swing at the swingin' tree.

Today, I sat there on the old, worn plank seat. Must be about four inches thick and was cut years and years ago by Old Pap.

That seat has been worn by many bottoms and bellies. It is shiny and smooth, and dark with age.

Bellies? You might wonder how it got worn by bellies. That makes me laugh as I think on it. I remembered that today while I was a-sittin' there, proper-like, just swingin' little swings back and forth.

I did lean way back, holdin' on to the ropes way up high-like. As I gazed up into the fall leaves, I remembered doin' that a million times as a child. I would lean as far back as I could and try to touch my head to the ground.

Now, that is an accomplishment for a small tyke, but for an old man like me? Well, today I didn't even try to touch my head to the ground, but I did enjoy rememberin'!

It was always fun to stand and turn the swing 'round and 'round, twistin' it up real tight. Then I would scrunch up into the seat on my belly, quick-like before it could unwind.

Then boy, would I have a ride whilst the swing unwound itself. I'd come off a laughin' and dizzy-like with my head spinnin' and all wobbly on my feet.

I would laugh and stumble 'til I fell flat into a pile of leaves or a big drift of snow, dependin' on the season. Sometimes it would be a mud puddle after spring thaw or maybe a summer rain, and then would Ma yell! Old Pap would say, "It's alright, Hannah! He's only a boy once!"

Today, I could almost hear the shouts and laughter of my friends and all the many young'uns who have played there over the years.

There was all Miss Dolly's girls, a-squealin' and a-laughin' with their pigtails flyin'. All my cousins and their young'uns in turn... so many happy voices over the years. Whether bottoms or bellies, swingin' was always fun.

One particular time I remember so clearly... so happened I was a-sittin' in the swing at the end of one sunny July day. All the young'uns from my Sunday School class and their families was there for a Sunday picnic under the big oaks there in the yard.

It was a boist'rous time for shore with all the games and good eatin' and swingin' higher than high. But what I remember most about that day was sittin' and gently swingin' whilst ever'one sat on stumps or on the ground on quilts and blankets.

It was gettin' on toward dusk and the fireflies was beginnin' to flit around. We was all a-singin' those wonderful old happy hymns together. Then, we was a-singin' the ones what declared our love for the Father. That night He seemed so close as the stars began to twinkle.

I purely want you to know that that was the night I understood what it truly meant to worship God. I was a-sittin' in that there swing and I worshiped from my heart-like.

I *knew* what it meant to adore God Almighty, to tell Him how I loved Him. *At last*, I really knew how truly mighty and *huge* He is! I opened my heart to Him in a way I never knew how to do before. My heart fairly sang with joy in the closeness I felt that night.

Did you know that when you truly worship God you feel closer to Him? Well, you do, and that's the truth of it.

Other swingin' times I would have a friend or cousin over and we would both sit on the heavy seat, facin' each other. We straddled one another, and it was always a game to see who could sit on top.

Anyhow, we would pump and pump. With both of us workin' our legs harder than hard, we could go high and fast!

Usually we would fall right out on the ground laughin' somethin' awful, all out of breath from the doin'. Then, iffen it was summer, we'd beg for some cool lemonade from Ma.

One really special time at that swing was the day it held my sweetheart, Isabel. I was behind her, gently swingin' her back and forth. I can still hear her skirts swishin' in the wind and see the little black toes of her shoes peekin' out from under there. I remember thinkin' she had the most beautiful tiny little feet I had ever seen. I had swung her before, but that day was different.

We was talkin' about nonsense mostly and dumb things like caterpillars and butterflies. She prob'ly wondered why the strange conversation. She even turned and looked a question up at me a time or two. You know how women do that, a-raisin' their eyebrows just so.

Do you know that a person can talk without sayin' nary a word? Well, they purely can.

I just kept pushin', and tryin' to find the words I was lookin' for, but for the life of me I couldn't find them. I was determined to "pop the question" that day, right there.

With me behind her back that way, I figgered for shore I could get up my courage-like. I was nervous and my hands was sweatin' rivers. I remember takin' 'em off the ropes one at a time and wipin' 'em on my pants there so's I wouldn't soil her purty pink dress.

I stumbled around, stammered and said all the wrong things. I never could even remember what words I used to ask her.

Then, suddenly I realized she'd got the message, 'cause she was right outa that there swingin' swing and in my arms, a-cryin' "Yes! Yes!"

Then we was twirlin' 'round and 'round. The swing whacked me right in the back of my knees and down we went, laughin' and cryin' for joy. We held on to each other like we could never let go! It was a wondrous day for both of us, to think we would be together always.

We had lotsa heart-to-heart talks there at the old swing, over the years. Me a-standin' behind a-pushin' and a-talkin' my way through my feelin's or a problem. Mostly she listened and agreed with whatever I would say.

Often, we would tease about the swingin' tree bein' like a tree of life, 'cause we often talked about life there. One of us would say to the other, "Wanna go out an' swing at the tree of life?" Then we would grin at each other and off we'd go.

We would talk about the good and the not-so-good times of life. And truth is, many times we talked about Scripture there.

Sometimes we even talked about that original Tree of Life.

You know, the one right there in Genesis, the first book in God's own Book. We'd talk how it might have been for Adam and Eve livin' in the Garden of Eden where that tree was. Or, we talked about how it will be in Heaven, where that Tree of Life will be.

I remember how we learn't verses in the Bible that talked about the righteous bein' a tree of life, and how the good things we say can be a tree of life. Verses like Proverbs 11:30 and Proverbs 15:4 are good ones!

God's Word is amazin'. My Isabel even found verses that said that wisdom is actually a tree of life. I will never ever forget that. It's in Proverbs, too. Chapter 3, verses 13-18.

Now and then, she would make a suggestion or a comment that would mean so much to me. Seems God would just plain put a wisdom in her that only a woman has.

Funny, I remember how she often used to talk out her feelin's and problems in my arms at night. In the quiet and dark of our room, it was always peaceful-like.

I 'specially remember nights when the window would be open, and the night air would stir the fluffy curtains she'd hung over the window there.

I'd hold her as she'd talk and gaze out the window at the stars. Sometimes we would just be quiet and listen to the frogs and crickets sing. She would open up then like at no other time. Those talkin' and sharin' times was very special times indeed.

Talkin' can open up your hearts to one 'nother. That way you have no secrets. You shorely get to know your own-self better and that person, too. You find out how they feel inside.

Sometimes, you even learn about your own-self when you are a-talkin' with God.

Did you know you can make all the difference in your marriage or even in a friendship simply by talkin' it out, even with the Lord God? Well, you can.

Old Pap and me had great fun at the swingin' tree over the years. He would swing me, pushin' gently at first just to get me started. Then as I would urge him with,

"Faster, Pap!" he would oblige and push harder and harder.

The faster I went, the higher I was. I could imagine that I was a bird a-flyin' there above the old cabin and the woods all around. I was never satisfied and sometimes I would beg, "Go under me, Pap!" Mostly he would say, "That's too high, Barney!"

But then one day he must have been in a really good mood and decided I was big enough, 'cause next thing I knew, he did! He went under me, a-pushin' the swing forward and higher than high as he ran underneath the plank seat! Wow! That was purely a ride to remember! He did that two or three times with me screechin' and laughin' with delight, hollerin' for more.

Suddenly as I swung back, there was Pap right under the swing, flat of his back, holdin' his sides and laughin' and laughin'.

He rolled out of the way of my feet just in time to keep from bein' kicked right in the side of his head. That was when I saw the blood. A lot of blood!

It scar't me somethin' awful seein' the blood there on the back of his head. You can bet I scrambled down faster than fast and fell to my knees at his side.

"Pap! Oh, Pap! Are you okay?" I found myself cryin' and couldn't understand his laughter. He was bleedin', and he might bleed nigh to death.

"Pap! Stop that! Stop that! You are bleedin' to death! Right here," I said as I put my hand against the back of his head.

"Owwww, Barney... what is it?" he asked between his gulpin' laughter, the tears runnin' down his face.

"You hurt yourself, Pap! Get up!"

Well, there I was a-scar't half out of myself. There he was lookin' at the blood on his hand and mine, and he was laughin'!

I thought he had knocked hisself crazy. I quick-jumped and ran for Ma, shoutin' to beat the band the whole way!

I brought her to his side. By then, he was sittin' up, and only chucklin', but still crazy, I thought.

"Pappy," she cried. "Are you okay?" She got the wet rag she had grabbed and squeezed the extry water out. She had dipped it in the bucket beside the door, and it had dripped all down her skirts. She didn't notice that at all, but began to gently bathe the back of Pap's head.

"Awww, that's okay, Hannah. I'm okay, just a little bump on the head is all. I must have knocked it against a rock. My foot slipped when I was runnin' back to give Barney here another push. I just fell is all," he said, as he pushed her hand away.

He said, "It can't be all that bad anyhow." Then he *really* saw the blood.

I remember it plain as plain when he saw the bloody rag. His face went white and he looked into her eyes with the oddest look on his face. "Well, I'll be! I did bump my noggin', didn't I?"

"Yes, Pappy, and you must get up. Come in and lie down right away!" I didn't often see my Ma cry, but she come awful near to it that day. Iffen he hadn't been so jolly about it all, I declare she would of for shore.

189

It turned out not to be serious after all, but did you know that when you get a cut on your head it can really bleed a lot? Well, it can. besides that, it can scare the life almost outa you, too!

Over the years there have been many dozens of young'uns playin' and swingin' at the old swingin' tree.

One day me and Isabel named that there tree. Ever after that, it was the "tree of life family tree."

All through the years, many young'uns have been a-climbin', a-jumpin', a-swingin', a-pushin', a-shoutin', a-laughin', a-runnin', and a-takin' on somethin' awful.

I guess I can safely say that no one else has ever been hurt at the swingin' tree 'sides Old Pap. Did you ever hear of anythin' so silly in all your life? Just a grandpa is the only one hurt outta all them that's played there.

13 Old Pap and His Larrupins

"O give thanks unto the Lord, for He is good:"
Psalm 107:1

Today, I heard an old codger at the cafe in town say somethin' I hadn't thought of in years. He was chowin' down on a big piece of pun'kin pie with three creamy scoops of vanilla ice cream.

I happened to be lookin' at him when he shut his eyes, smacked his lips, and said, "Mmmm, that's larrupin'!"

Oh, did that take me back! I remember Pap sayin' that so many times when I was a boy. He told the most wondrous story of how he learn't that word. The truth is that I can still see the sparkle right in his eyes when I remember the tellin' of it!

He said he learn't it from a true-to-life cowboy. Now, to my notion, cowboys was as mysterious as Injuns, which is what I called 'em back then. And I was plumb delighted to hear that my very own Pap had met one and actually been friends with a true-to-life cowboy! A real live one!

He told how this old bow-legged cowboy come along one day on our little homestead. In the cabin where I really and truly lived as a boy years later, after my Pa had passed on. Right where Old Pap lived.

It was a wondrous thing to think that I could really breathe the same air and walk on the same ground and sit on the same porch as a real-to-life cowboy!

By the time Cowboy Jim showed up, Henrietta was gone, but my Ma was still there as one of three young'uns that Pap and his mama, Gram, was raisin'. Those young'uns was up and runnin', and they was hard put to keep up with 'em.

Ma would smile years later as Pap would tell of the day Jim come a-walkin' up with his legs all bowed out, a-shufflin' from side to side and chewin' on a big wad of tobacca. Pap said that they sat there on the porch a good spell whilst Cowboy Jim told all kinds of stories about his round-up, trail-drivin' days down South.

After a while, Ma had said, "Pappy, Gram has supper ready," and they went in and gathered 'round the big table there.

Of course, Jim declared he didn't need a thing to eat and that she shouldn't have bothered, but they both always said they never, ever saw a person that could pack away a meal like old Cowboy Jim could! And him as skinny as a rail.

Gram had a steamin' kettle of her beef stew, and she had made those little fluffy biscuits. The ones that pulled apart and made steam that smelled like they come straight from heaven. I dunno as I ever ate any biscuits anywhere just like my Gram and my Ma made. 'Course, Ma learn't from Gram, accordin' to Old Pap. Isabel learn't from Ma.

Well, that day, whilst ever'one watched in amazement, Cowboy Jim ate and ate and ate. Harry, Hank, and my Ma, Hannah, sat there with their mouths open, accordin' to Pap. He said they wouldn't of got a bite but for Gram a-spoonin' some into their bowls where it grew cold in their watchin' the old cowboy. He ate more food than anybody!

Finally, he sat back after a hot piece of fresh apple pie, rubbed his belly, and burped a big old burp. Then they started to giggle, a-shovin' their hands in their mouths.

But what did them in was when he said, "Mmmm- mmm, that was larrupin!!"

Then the silence was plumb broken as the three young'uns really started a-gigglin'. Then they was a-laughin' right out and holdin' their sides. They tried to leave the table in all their embarrassment.

No one had ever heard that word, and it struck them all so funny. But, by then, the grownups was a-laughin' too, and Cowboy Jim was the loudest. Old Pap always said it was the most fun they'd all had since the circus clowns passed through the year before.

Tellin' it, he would laugh outright, and ever' time he did that Happy would jump to his feet and wag that little tail as hard as he could. It was like he was a-laughin', too!

After that, "larrupin'" was Old Pap's favorite word to use to describe anythin' he loved to eat. It could be a fresh cherry tomato he popped into his mouth at the garden, or a big bowl of popcorn enjoyed on the porch of an evenin'.

I loved to see Ma's eyes light up when he said, "That's larrupin'!" Then she would say, "Aw, Pappy…" The truth was that she purely loved to see him enjoy life. Especially when he was on up in his years.

You know, I always took that to mean Old Pap was thankful. He taught me to always be thankful for all my blessin's. Eatin' somethin' delicious was shorely a blessin' all right.

So, I began to think of that strange word larrupin' to mean "Thank you, Lord, for this delicious food!" I remember laughin' right out loud in my bed one night when I thought that up.

Why, when I said my prayers after that, I even imagined Jesus there a-throwin' his head back a-laughin' with me.

Ever after that night when I would count my blessin's, I would end the list with a smile and say, "Lord, that was larrupin'."

14 Old Pap and Butterfly Memories

"And when they were come, and had gathered the church
together, they rehearsed all that God had done with them..."
Acts 14:27a

I was sittin' on a big old stump over in the woods near the garden today. It was pleasant and the air smelled delicious.

I know for a fact it was a really old stump, 'cause I can remember clearly sittin' there when I was a boy. I would have to rest a spell after a-follerin' Old Pap up and down the long rows in the garden there. It's a-gettin' pretty rotten these days.

Years later, I was still hard-pressed to keep up with him, even with his limp. He was a hearty old soul, he was. I guess him keepin' active kept him strong-like. I truly do believe that bein' busy helped old Happy Hopscotch, too. He follered Old Pap ever'wheres, and he stayed strong like Old Pap did. They might of slowed some, but they both was busy.

Did you know that the more you keep busy, the more you feel like keepin' busy? Well, you do. That is the truth of it.

Anyway, today I was just a-sittin' there restin' my bones. A little orange butterfly rested on the knee of my overhauls. Just sat there for the longest time, purty as you please.

Purty soon, another one stopped by. It just touched down and went right on its way. Then I noticed there was a lot of them little critters out today.

One would light on my sleeve or the scuffed toe of my old work boots. Some would stay a while. Others only flitted along, touchin' down like an airplane and takin' right off again.

It come to me that butterflies is like memories, or that memories is like butterflies. Whichever it is, they come and they go.

They bless you or sometimes they bring back hurts for just a moment. Time and the good Lord eases the pain, of course, but the memory of it is still there.

Just like a butterfly, memories are each different. Some may seem alike, but deep down, there are differences.

I guess iffen I was to choose, I would say the memories I love most are the ones what are filled with the Lord and His goodness. Like the first memory in this book, when I truly believed.

Of course, Old Pap always said God tells us in His own Book to rehearse what the Lord has done, so I purely love to do that. It lifts me right up.

Did you know that when you tell what the Lord has done in your own life, it makes you feel a right-smart better? Well, it shorely does!

So, iffen you find your own-self enjoyin' these butterfly memories of mine, then it was a good thing to put them down into a book. I pray God touches your heart in some way through my very own butterfly memories.

THE END

COMING SOON:

"Old Pap's Recipe Collection"

The next Old Pap book will be
Old Pap's very own personal
recipe collection.
It is co-authored by a
grandma, Jane Priest Wilson, and
her *granddaughter*, Rebecca Gunn.
This unique recipe book is
co-illustrated by a
grandpa, John W. Wilson, and his
granddaughter, Sarah Gunn.
We know that family is a precious
gift from the Lord, and it is a
great privilege for
families to work together.
Be watching for this most unique,
fun *country recipe book*
in the near future!

Supplemental
Grammar

Supplemental Grammar

Circle any correct sentences:

1. Old Pap told me that she would say, "There is not a man yet that can whiten the laundry properly."

2. I have always wisht I could ask that dog a few questions.

3. Then the silence was plumb broken as the three young'uns really started a-gigglin', and then they was a-laughin' right out and holdin' their sides.

4. Tonight I had me a mess of fish for supper.

5. I was nearly frozen when I got back inside. Now, I have the chores done for the day, and a good hot mug of coffee is warming me right up.

6. Me and Old Pap walked ever'where we went.

7. Old Pap told me she'd say, "Ain't a man yet what can do up a whitenin' wash proper-like."

8. It was springtime and a good while until school would even start.

9. I got up a minute ago and wiped a big circle in the frost on the window so's I could see out.

10. But, that evening she slowed down, and I looked up over my reading glasses.

11. Then the silence was completely broken as the three children really started to giggle. Soon, they were laughing out loud and holding their sides.

12. I am so thankful that Old Pap taught me young to cast my cares on the Lord.

13. She was laying on her side, and they were climbing all over themselves and all over each other while trying to find a place to eat.

14. I have always wished I could ask that dog a few questions.

15. I had a mess of fish for supper tonight.

16. Then we were singing the ones that declared our love for the Father.

17. I am so thankful that Old Pap taught me when I was young to cast my cares on the Lord.

18. There are a lot of ways to make a snowman into a person.

19. I did lean way back, holding on to the ropes way up high.

20. But that evenin', she slows down and I looks up over my readin' glasses.

About the Author

About the Author

Jane Priest Wilson is a Christian author who has been writing seriously since high school. She was a columnist and feature writer for two newspapers and has written ministry newsletters for more than twenty-five years. Jane also has numerous *works in progress*, which include a second novel. She has written stories about deaf children and other children's stories, a children's chapter book, and other various writing projects.

 Jane and her husband, John, are also writing about their many experiences in various ministries through the years since their ministry began in 1988. Some of their stories include experiences in which they saw things like a woman being killed at a post office, the true story of "The Machete Brothers." There is also the adventurous story about the summer they sang gospel music and conducted Sunday services in an Alaska Highway café in the Yukon. There are also many tales to relate about pastoring churches, ministering in dozens of nursing homes, while traveling on the road as music evangelists, which is what they are currently doing. They began their travels in a converted school bus years ago. Having seven flat tires in one trip was not fun! There

are good and bad things that happen along the way, and inspiring one-on-one experiences that are worth sharing with others.

John and Jane married as high school sweethearts forty-seven years ago. She is thankful for his tremendous encouragement to her in her writing. They raised their two awesome children, Jimmy and Lara, and now have four wonderful grandchildren! Serving the Lord and times with family are their greatest joys in life.

In 2012 Jane's first book, _Miracle in Madison: an Inspirational Suspense Novel_ was published. She started writing it in 1978 when they were dreaming of moving to the woods and living off the land with their children. They were seeking peace and tranquility in their lives. Ten years later, their dream had come true in the woods of Minnesota, and they had found that peace through the Lord Jesus Christ.

The book was finished just before starting in the ministry in 1988. Of course, after having given her life totally to Jesus Christ, it was re-written to make this mystery book into an "inspirational suspense novel". It is their earnest prayer that you will draw closer to the living God through the telling of that tale.

The following is a peek at the first page of Miracle in Madison:

Preview: Miracle in Madison

Chapter 1

Far away in the forest the big man furtively maneuvered among the trees. He had a sinister way about him as he made his plans, constantly looking from side to side, then behind him as well. His feet shuffled through the leaves that had begun to fall to the forest floor. His mind was filled with the intent of his heart and he determined to do whatever it took to make his plan work…. anything… yes, anything. He tugged his hat lower on his forehead as he doggedly pushed his way through the brush.

***

Susan Greyson had been very happy that day in the early fall of 1978. Tragedy was impending, and she would have done things differently if she had only known. The water was crystal clear and ice cold. The fish swimming against the current made a silvery reflection. The morning air was fresh and clean, and the gentle breeze rustled the forest leaves.

These are probably the happiest days of my life, she thought, drawing her knees up to her chin. She gazed into the sparkling mountain stream, absorbing the beauty around her. Every sound was like music to her ears. She could hear birds singing playfully to each other. Above their song, she could hear the chattering of two red squirrels fussing over a nut. When Susan looked, she found the smallest one had a beautiful, bushy tail, and the other had a merry twinkle in his eyes. There was a raccoon across the stream peeking around a bush at her.

WATCH FOR:

Miracle on the Mountain
(sequel to
Miracle in Madison)

23546644R00118

Made in the USA
Lexington, KY
17 June 2013